# CEREMONY OF INNOCENCE

*Books by James Forman*

MY ENEMY, MY BROTHER

CEREMONY OF INNOCENCE

# CEREMONY
# OF
# INNOCENCE

*by*
*JAMES FORMAN*

HAWTHORN BOOKS, INC. *Publishers*

*This book is for Hans and Sophie Scholl. It is also for a staunch little school that I attended during the years of their conspiracy, The Vincent Smith School, light-years removed from Nazi Germany, and for the school's three sturdy pillars: Miss Adelaide V. Smith, Miss Nellora A. Reeder, and Mr. Lawrence Mitchell.*

CEREMONY OF INNOCENCE

CHAPTER ONE

● Sophie walked so sedately to the Gestapo car that the watching students said later either she was not human, or she did not understand what was happening.

The short drive down the Ludwigstrasse was prolonged briefly by bomb damage to the pavement, and then she cried. It was the only time she broke down. "Alex, Alex," she mourned.

Hans felt nothing. This seemed to have happened to him many times before, and he looked out through blind eyes at students walking on their way to class. He had failed. If the leaflets had been ready a week before . . . if the classroom doors had not been locked . . . Perhaps it was never meant to end any other way.

There were only a few more blocks to the mounted statue of Ludwig, the beloved mad King of Bavaria. Behind his statue rose the formal yellow eighteenth-century facade of the Wittelsbacher Palace. It looked oddly flat under the

3

hard blue sky, like a cardboard stage set raised to intimidate passers-by.

The square was quiet when the car drew up. Sophie squeezed Hans's hand as they got out. She had completely recovered herself. Her eyes were bright and unwinking, and she moved toward Gestapo headquarters as proudly as a princess on her way to a coronation. Close beside her, Hans looked like a thoughtful student with an examination in prospect. His hands were plunged deep into his jacket pockets. It was the left one that sent back the first warning to his brain. A hard knot of forgotten paper: Christl's draft! In the moments that remained, his fingers worked to obliterate it, struggling like snakes in the dark.

Up three stone steps, and the prisoners under guard entered Gestapo headquarters. The marble floor of the corridor echoed. Its bare walls had been recently whitewashed to an off-white creamy shade, pinkly tinctured as though the cow had been left too long without milking. A guard stood beside a wooden bench where a row of silent people waited. Most of them kept their heads bowed, their eyes intently upon the floor.

"Say nothing," Hans whispered to Sophie as they passed the long bench. "We'll get through this somehow."

"No talking!" A hand clapped him on the shoulder. "And keep moving. Down to the end and turn left."

The receiving room was on the ground floor. Like the corridor, it was essentially bare: one desk, a filing cabinet, and three chairs occupied by two men in uniform and one in civilian clothes. The men were examining papers, and for some time Hans and Sophie were ignored. As Hans became accustomed to the bright light that shone from above and behind the desk, he realized that the room was

4

not as immaculate as it had first seemed. There were lighter areas on the walls, where pictures had been removed and only partially filled with portraits of Hitler and Goering. A framed photograph of Il Duce stood awkwardly in the corner, a crack across the glass as though it had fallen. A talcum of plaster dust shaken down by recent air raids covered the floor.

"Hans and Sophie Scholl?" It was the civilian who spoke. They admitted that much.

"You are accused of treason against the State."

The only reply was Hans's cough. If he could only manage to get his hand to his mouth . . . a hand full of scraps from the incriminating document.

Undeterred by Hans's silence, his questioner perused a sheet of paper, one of the leaflets from the University. "This," he said, "speaks of German youth claiming its personal freedom, German youth settling accounts. And listen to this! 'Awake, my people! The beacons are aflame!' How poetic. Did you steal that from Schiller? Come now; you did write it."

Again Hans said nothing. He had managed to move some of the paper from his pocket into his mouth. Trying to swallow, he coughed again.

"Yes, I believe I too would cough with embarrassment if I had written that," said his questioner. " 'Students, the eyes of the German people are upon us.' You are wrong there, Scholl. Tragically wrong." He balled up the leaflet and dropped it into a wire wastebasket. "I think you are Aryan, Scholl. You look it. Have you Jewish friends?"

"No, none," Hans lied, hoping to protect them.

"There is something wrong with you, something twisted. What is it? Have you tuberculosis? The way you are cough-

5

ing . . . Surely you didn't think this outburst would cause any real trouble. Some conspirators you are, running about as if you were throwing confetti at a masquerade party. I am ashamed of you. Bock, Drexler, take these two away." The SS guards approached. "And see what it is Scholl has in his mouth."

Hans pulled away, trying to swallow. Hands were laid on him, forcing him down. Stars burst inside his brain as his head hit the floor.

"We only have to use a stomach pump, Scholl."

Still he hung on, chewing.

"Give me a pen, someone." As Hans lay flat on the floor, two fountain pens, blunt ends foremost, pressed into his cheeks agonizingly, forcing his jaws apart. "There, that does it. Get up, Scholl. Someone help him up."

Those soggy scraps, the few bits of paper still in his pocket, his belt, shoelaces, tie—all personal effects were taken and placed in a large brown envelope. Sophie, too, was searched. She had nothing.

"You will get all this back in due course," Hans was told. "You, or, more likely, your next of kin. Take them away."

Separated from his sister without a chance for a parting word, Hans was prodded down to a long basement corridor where the damp air smelled of mildew and sweat. He passed many doors, all closed, mostly on silent rooms. But from behind one door rose a high-pitched cry; no human sound, but the noise a dog makes when it has been run over.

"Am I permitted to go to the lavatory?" he asked.

His guards seemed not to have heard him. They pushed

him roughly along for a few more yards, then showed him into a small room. A toilet was there, and Hans closed the door behind him. They were waiting outside when he had finished.

"It's broken," he told them.

"What do you mean, broken?" Until now, neither guard had spoken a word.

"I mean that I flushed it," Hans explained, "and the water went all the way down. Then it started coming up, and well, look. It isn't stopping."

Already there was water in the corridor.

"Move along, Scholl. Move! You don't seem to realize the seriousness of your situation." Hans received a shove for emphasis, which brought him up short before a stout metal door. It was locked with an ancient lock, older, it would seem, than the rest of the building. One guard inserted a large key into the mechanism. It turned with a crunching sound as though he had broken his wrist in forcing the lock. With the screech and the ringing thump of a gunshot, the latch complied. Hans was pushed inside: sink, wooden swing-down shelf and bedroll, walls etched with graffiti, a window close to the ceiling, one bare bulb overhead. Before he could turn around, the great door had clanged behind him, seeming to close forever on sunlight and hope. He was entombed.

A vast block of granite and iron was piled above him. There were other cells, above and below, uncounted numbers of them. How many Germans had occupied this cell before him? How many had been tormented here? How many were dead now, without leaving a trace beyond their scribblings on these walls? There were Jewish names next to prayers and curses, beneath pleas to let someone

7

know that they had been here. There were dates as well, years old in the case of the Jewish names. Hans had heard that Jews were no longer honored with interrogation, those few that survived. He'd had Jewish neighbors once. Now their apartments were occupied by strangers, boarded up, or, in some cases, burned to the ground. Others, Aryan by party definition, had vanished: killed at the front or at home by the bombs, or taken to concentration camps for calling Goering a fool. Hans's own father had been imprisoned once for saying in public that Hitler was a scourge against God; after three months in prison, he was freed—with no marks on his body, but a wound in his soul that would not heal.

Hans himself had known prison before.

As a teenager he had been a member of the Jungenschaft, a group of boys who dared to read foreign books and sing Russian folk songs. For this he had gone to jail. The activities of the Jungenschaft seemed laughably trivial now, but it had been deadly serious seven years ago, when he was seventeen.

The prison to which they had taken him then had not been in Ulm, nor at Dachau, thank God, which the prison van had passed on the autobahn. It had been here in Munich, the old Stadelheim Prison. Even then Stadelheim had a bad reputation, and Hans had pictured himself spitting the bloody stumps of his teeth one by one into a rusty can. He had not been tortured, but had been locked in a dreary cell at the end of another long corridor. A death cell, surely, from which he would be dragged struggling like a butterfly dying in a bottle. He had wondered how it would be to feel the scorching hail of bullets through his body. But no priest had come

8

to him. Instead, the warden had appeared with a plate of food. A jolly man. "Delicious!" he had said. "Eat up. From this prison we send them to the block plump as pullets." So throughout that night Hans had felt the knife crushing against the back of his neck. But the whole thing was nothing but a show to frighten misbehaving boys. Two weeks of watching cloud patterns beyond a small window, of reading tedious party literature because there was nothing else to do, and they had let him go with a contemptuous lecture. "No more non-Aryan songs about 'nut-brown maids.' No more reading forbidden books. No more disrespectful comments in public places. No, no more foolishness," Hans had agreed submissively, and he had been given a ticket home to Ulm by third-class coach.

Liberated prisoners were supposed to run for dark places to escape the crowding sky, but Hans had wanted to bathe in light; he wanted to embrace the whole world— its sounds, its tastes, its colors. With luck, he could expect half a century of savoring. Fifty years was little enough. He needed a thousand years.

His mother had wept at the first sight of him. He was all skin and bones. "Lean and fit, Mother. I'm just lean and fit."

"Hans, you look fine," his father had insisted, adding on the side, "I'm proud of you, son, but you won't do this again, will you? If you knew how your mother has suffered . . ."

"That's a pledge, Father," Hans had replied with total conviction.

Only Sophie had questioned. "You didn't mean what you promised Father, did you, Hans?"

9

"I don't know what you're talking about, Sophie. I honestly don't." Hans had felt Sophie was cut off from the realities of life. Lately she had been reading poetry aloud to herself in a low murmuring voice, little introspective pieces that she had composed but which were seldom displayed. Still, it was Sophie to whom he could talk freely, and she listened as she had always listened, with her upper lip slightly raised as if to interrupt. But, as always, she had heard him through: how he intended to keep his mouth shut, his books hidden, and himself out of trouble. He was no crusader and never would be, and all he wanted from the Nazi party was to be left alone. Not once did she question or contradict; but when he had finished she opened a well-thumbed book and pointed to his fresh handwriting on the flyleaf. In black ink, the single sentence read, "Tear the hearts from our bodies, and you will scorch your fingers on them."

"I wrote that long ago," he told her. But it wasn't so, and she knew it. Somehow Sophie always knew.

Now, as Hans waited in his cell beneath the Wittelsbacher Palace, he wondered if it wouldn't have been better if they had tortured him seven years ago. A few teeth in a tin can, and perhaps he wouldn't be here now. He opened his mouth slowly and closed it again, testing the ache in his jawbones where the fountain pens had prodded.

The interrogators, whom he had been expecting all morning, came in midafternoon, heralded by the dire clanging of the iron door. With them came the usual paraphernalia he had come to expect: hard-backed chairs and a metal tripod bearing a reflector lamp, which they set up silently and laboriously. Presently the lamp burst on, gilding the cell with a bitter, highly concentrated light. The voice that pierced through the radiance was as harsh as the sudden glare.

"So you're a student, Scholl. One of those intellectuals, a superior type. I always enjoy chatting with scholars." The great body of a man leaned over him. Hans could smell his sour breath, but at first he could not make out his features. When his eyes had become adjusted to the glare, he saw that the face was not an unpleasant one. The eyebrows slanted comically toward the temples, and the eyes seemed warm and guileless, the mouth full and weak. Only the man's nose was ugly. It was pitted with dark holes, and the left nostril had been ripped free years before and had imperfectly healed.

After a few preliminary questions, which Hans refused to answer, the second interrogator took over. A cold wisp of a man, he projected an image of unrelenting blackness. He did not approach his quarry as the other had, but stalked the corners of the room suspiciously, as though expecting sudden treachery. His voice floated, like oil on water. It was utterly calm, amused and cordial, with a hint of education. For some time he quizzed Hans as a friend, with fond curiosity, it would seem. Hans gave no answers. "You should realize it is useless to conceal anything. We know all about you. Yes, everything." He turned upon Hans a face like a politely inquisitive hatchet.

Hours passed. The men took turns. They refreshed themselves with coffee and cigarettes, offering some to Hans. The air whirled with smoke. When the first man took over again, his manner had changed. Rough and

11

stubbled as his red-bristled chin, his voice barked out, a Gestapo technique Hans had heard described as *anschnauzen*, "snorting." Would he confess? To what, he was never asked. Would he sign this paper voluntarily? A paper he was not allowed to read. Hans scarcely heard the shouting. It was the full lips, open and wet at the corners, that fascinated him. Like groping leeches, they were after his blood.

In a weird and disembodied fashion, Hans was fascinated. He studied the face pressed close to his as impersonally as he would study a mountain landscape. Where did such passion come from? How could it be maintained hour after hour? Something was wrong with the man's eyes. One had closed to a slit in the strong light. The other was wide open, the sleepless eye of a lynx. Then he realized that it was a glass eye. Gradually the pace of the interrogation increased. A question was asked repetitively and then dropped. Another was asked several times, then another, until the series began again. Every word was shouted, while the terrible eye bored into him. Under the light his own eyes felt as if suction cups were pulling them from behind. Yet he knew he could hold out. From time to time the interrogator rasped his unshaven chin with his thumb. He put a finger into his ear and shook his head. He was not a young man, and he was getting tired. Hans felt like trying to cheer him up, but was too disengaged to make the effort.

Hans judged it to be morning again by the trace of pallid light in the window. He was rather surprised that so much time had passed without the interrogators resorting to physical coercion.

The thin man spoke from behind him. "I think, young

12

man, you had better realize that you will never leave this place until you have told us what you know. You're a bright student, undoubtedly; a Bohemian intellectual, but that does not entitle you to strike at the State with impunity. Should we spank you and send you home to your mother? If only the Führer had your sense of humor." There was a chilling joviality in his tone. "Scholl— your first name is Hans, isn't it? Hans, I'm old enough to be your father. I'm not a ruthless man, whatever you may think. But our National Socialist dream, if it is to become a reality, demands certain incidental inhumanities. Hans, I take it you're not Jewish, but I believe you have Jewish friends."

"I thought all the Jews were dead," Hans told him.

"Not dead, my boy. Uprooted. Transplanted. We are gardeners, Hans. National Socialism is our garden. We uproot, and transplant the weeds so that the flowers may flourish. But we are busy gardeners, Hans. We have only so much time for each weed."

"What my colleague means," interrupted the heavy man, "is that we can teach you things about pain unknown even to medical students such as yourself."

"I'm not afraid of you," Hans said, addressing them directly for the first time. "It's you who are afraid of me." And it was true. He had passed beyond fear into fantasy, and their words had all the implausibility of a nightmare.

"Is that the way it looks to you?" The large man rubbed the top of Hans's head with his fist, softly, as if he were soothing a dog.

"If you torture me, I may sign anything you place before me," Hans said, "but tomorrow I will recant."

13

He would admit anything about himself, but never must he implicate Sophie or the others.

Whether they intended merely to frighten him or to administer the most subtle of tortures Hans was not to know, for a third man entered the room, carrying a briefcase full of documents. The other two examined the papers, and then the fat one turned to Hans. He spoke peevishly. "My dear boy, you should have told us. The time and trouble we would have been saved! Your apartment is a treasure house. That wastebasket is better than any statement you could make. How you got away with this business for so long is amazing. I can't imagine even you took it seriously. Was it some sort of—what is the word . . . *avant-garde*, that's it—*avant-garde* prank? Truthfully, my boy, were you never concerned? Did you never weigh the consequences? Surely you must occasionally have been afraid."

"Always," Hans admitted. "I can't remember not being afraid."

"Well," inserted the slender interrogator, "we will leave you to relax, Hans, while we digest this new material. But keep in mind this is not a game you stop playing when you're about to lose. You cannot as children do, shout 'Time.' "

With this the three men departed. For a moment after the heavy door had slammed, the cell echoed with a metallic clangor. Then everything was quiet.

Time, Hans thought. Yes, children could shout "Time," and call off the consequences, but he had never had such delusions. Always he had known, and always he had been afraid. Exultant sometimes, hopeful, laughing—but always there had been fear.

Even last spring, a balmy time in Munich, a time for street-corner conversations, a time for studying with windows flung open to the scent of flowers, even then there had been fear.

The war had still been a far-off thing, a newspaper and news-reel war. Rommel was at the gates of Cairo. He was about to break through the British lines and capture their empire at El Alamain; and in Russia the Sixth Army had been massing for the last great "Home for Christmas" offensive.

But by then Hans no longer read the newspapers. He had no time for movies. He worked late, behind locked doors. With Sophie and Alex he discussed and formulated and wrote down words that might send all three to the executioner's block. Christl was the only other person who knew what they were doing. He had offered to help, but Hans declined, because Christl was a husband and a father twice over. Hans should have kept Sophie out of it too, but when it came to faith and willpower, she was more than a match for anyone. That part of Hans which was reluctant and afraid needed her almost motherly support. Of the trio, Alex was undoubtedly the most natural conspirator. He would risk his life daily and with gaiety as long as he had a gambler's chance. But it was Hans, as author of the pamphlets, who combined his own views with those of Goethe, Schiller, and Lao-tse, and bound them together. Hans had none of Sophie's indestructable conviction and little of Alex's careless courage, and it was all he could do to hide his fears lest he infect the others.

Drops of perspiration trickled down his temples as he wrote and rewrote that second leaflet. He called on the intellectuals to find one another, to unite and cut away the Nazi cancer. He condemned the deportation of the Jews. "We are all guilty, guilty, guilty!" he wrote, and ended, as he had before, with a request that the leaflets be copied and passed on.

Once the pamphlet had been discussed and revised, the three of them had gathered around the copy machine like clandestine surgeons officiating at an illegal abortion. Though his companions seemed calm, every footfall startled Hans. A mouse gnawing in the wall was enough to make his fingers unsteady. After four weary nights of printing, he had learned to bear tension, but the task of circulating the pamphlets through the shadow-haunted streets of Munich remained.

"Before we go, promise to marry me," Alex said.

"Ouch! I'll promise if you let go of my ears," said Sophie.

"Promise first."

"I promise. You sadist! You ought to cut your fingernails."

"Come on, idiots. To work." Hans divided the bundle of leaflets among them.

They went separately, at one-minute intervals, so as not to be caught together. Sophie went first, and waved from the foot of the long stairwell. Then Alex went, bounding off as though on his way to a class picnic. Alone, Hans took deep, slow breaths as his wristwatch tolled the slow seconds. "Now, Hans," he whispered, and took a jerky step. His skeleton felt as if rigged on strings, his heart beat out a message of terror. "If fear were the best guarantee of a long life," he told him-

16

self, "I'd live to be a thousand." Somewhere a clock struck two, and he felt each bombination like an electric shock. Time was flying. Hurry, hurry, down the side streets of one of the largest cities in one of the largest empires on the planet earth as it hurtles down the void somewhere or nowhere. Hans felt every mile of the long descent. Was his executioner standing behind that blank door? Were footfalls following, matched to his own? He stopped, forcing himself to breathe slowly, giving his nerves time to settle and his brain a chance to clear. "Have you gone mad?" he asked himself. To think there was any use shoving fatuous bits of paper into the mail slots of strangers! To imagine that this might unseat a tyrant who had conquered half of Europe! He froze before a hundred shadows, and he resolved to make this the last leaflet.

Sophie was waiting for him when he reached home. She stood at the head of the stairs holding a candle that threw out a frail halo of light, and she looked enviably calm. He felt a moment's resentment toward his sister for her lack of fear, then propelled himself up steps which seemed vertical, each one three feet high.

"Hans, what took you so long? You're exhausted." He denied this. "Well, you look grubby. Here, use this." She offered a handkerchief.

"I haven't a cold, Sophie."

"You're sweating. Well, anyway, your forehead's damp."

How shamefully his body betrayed him.

"Poor Hans. All the real burdens are yours. I wish I could do more to help you." When she offered him something for a headache, he denied having one. "Here's a glass of water and some aspirin," she persisted. "They'll do you good."

"Stop mothering me, Sophie," he said, but, still protesting, swallowed the aspirin.

That was only the first night of distribution. It took two more to get rid of the original leaflets, and while habit tended to repair Hans's nerves, weariness increasingly frayed them. He could not sleep. Sophie slept easily. She seemed to welcome sleep, but Hans fought it off as he would have fought off death. No matter what had gone on before or might happen in the future, Sophie could lie down, close her eyes, and drift into unconsciousness, smiling up from her pillow like a wise goddess. Hans simply could not understand her. His toes would stretch themselves until they touched the rail at the foot of the bed, a kind of iron assurance that he could not fall through the thin mattress. Then, during the final moment of consciousness, as he was congratulating himself on falling asleep, he would be jolted fully awake again, his heart beating like a trip-hammer. Behind his shut lids lights would jump, and he could not bear to open them for fear of really seeing the terrifying image that threatened him behind closed eyes: a black-clad figure beside his bed. When he finally slept, it was never for more than an hour or two. Usually one of his "red" dreams would wake him up for good. Then he would lie there wondering about the difference between him and his sister, wondering how Sophie could sleep so soundly, why she approached the dangerous task of distributing their leaflets so fearlessly and without doubt. For one thing, he decided, she had no imag-

18

ination. But however vindictive his private thoughts, in the end he always reached one amazed conclusion: Sophie knew she would live forever. She knew this with her whole body. Painlessly, she would pass from this life to a better one, while he knew deep down that one day, sooner or later, life for him would end. He had seen it end for countless patients, with never any indication that it might go on in some other form.

After the third of these restless nights, he rose with the first light. Ersatz coffee was small comfort. He gulped down two cups while trying to glean something from his neglected medical books. Before he left for his first class, he woke Sophie. She sat up with a smile. No shrouded figure had stood beside her bed.

"Oh, such a peaceful night," she said. "But what about you, Hans? Did you sleep well?"

"All right, thanks, toward morning," he lied. "Sophie, do you believe in dreams?" She said she never dreamed, but he knew this wasn't true. As a child she had often spoken of dreams as if they were real. Visiting a friend, he had once heard her say, "I was here last night and played with you." To Hans, dreams were real; a dream might be a veiled reality or the revelation of a secret truth about a person. He was frightened by his blood-red dreams which had occurred since the time in his childhood when his father had sent him to the woodpile to destroy an injured chicken. The dreams frightened him so much that he could not talk about them directly.

"Why do we take such chances, Sophie?" he asked. "Are we out of our minds?"

She answered that God would guide them, offering him a prop upon which he could not lean. "Hans, all over Munich they'll be reading what you wrote. Your words, Hans. It makes me proud to know that, and most of them will know that you are right. We can't stop now. They depend on us." Her voice was vibrant with enthusiasm.

"We may have no choice," he replied. "There's talk a student medical corps will be sent to the front after this term." The news silenced Sophie. With arms hugged together, she walked to the window.

The news had shocked him, too, at first, and yet he could not analyze his reactions entirely. Certainly it was only a substitution of hazards. But once he got used to the idea, Hans had caught himself singing; not with happiness, but from mental relief.

Sophie turned abruptly from the glass. "That's all the more reason for pressing on now." She was no dreamer. She knew their weapons were blunt ones at best. Now they had only courage and truth. Even time was running out. Everything they had done was useless if they did not push on. "We must print extra copies, right now," she insisted. He put her off until classes were over for the day. Then they printed leaflets far into the night, finally sleeping only so they would have strength, when dark came again, to distribute their dangerous ideas.

With a bundle of leaflets under her coat, Sophie gave him a reassuring hug. "Take care," was the last thing she said to him.

"You, too," Hans replied. More than once during the terrible hours that followed he found himself faintly smiling at this innocent exchange.

As he watched his sister depart into the night, he thought that only a woman as strong, or perhaps as blind,

20

as Sophie, could remain outwardly serene on such a mission. Without a backward glance, she was on her way to the railroad station to join Alex. Together they would journey to Stuttgart and Ulm, carrying leaflets to new horizons.

Hans had the task of distributing the leaflets in Munich alone. By now the police would be alerted. It crossed his mind to tear up the pamphlets and go to bed. Finally he went into the streets, responding in every nerve to the jangle of a doorbell in the dark, to the faceless occupants of a parked car, to the flicker of a flashlight in a side street. By four in the morning only a few leaflets remained. The empty city echoed to the slightest sound. His breath resounded like a bellows. A pamphlet slid under a door rasped like a saw, yet no sound prepared him for the blinding light which suddenly beamed down the building opposite, swept across the cobbled street and transfixed him with his fistful of leaflets. Hans stood in the glare for a second, big and helpless as a snowman in the white light, then he leaped forward with the patrol car's searchlight following him.

"Halt!"

The sharp command was repeated once and then firing began. Bullets sparked from the cobbles as Hans lurched into a narrow alley, fell scrabbling, lost several leaflets, and plunged on again. Bent low, touching the dark walls for guidance, he pounded along the alley. Nothing human barred his way, but suddenly he was halted by a six-foot-high brick wall topped with broken bottles. The police car had stopped at the alley's mouth. Strident voices, bobbing flashlights pursued him, so he went over the wall, the glass scything into his left hand and tearing

21

his coat. He raced around countless corners, sprinted through dark alleys, and finally halted, his lungs on fire, in a familiar street. The lights showed the blood welling out red from between the fingers of his clenched hand. Hans wrestled his coat off and wrapped it around the wounds, then stumbled on again.

Hans never knew how long it took him to reach home. He leaned against the closed door and felt faint with relief and loss of blood. Fireworks played under his lids when he closed his eyes, but urgent things remained to be done. His coat might have left telltale threads on the wall. His trousers, too, were torn, so in the end he burned all his clothes before he dared lie down. Several times he had to sit with his head between his knees. "God, let me finish. Let me finish quickly, before they knock." Light was appearing outside when he finally lay down on his bed with his hand wrapped in white gauze, far too exhausted to await the fatal rapping he knew must come.

The midday sun was streaming in at the window when loud knocking woke him from a sound sleep. In a panic he went to the door, turned the key, which he had left in the lock, and found Sophie standing on the threshold, bright as a knife that shows no sign of wear.

"Hans, it went beautifully!" she exclaimed. "Alex was splendid. You should have seen him. The most fantastic poise . . . but Hans, your fingers!" She took his bandaged hand in hers as though it were a hurt bird.

"What happened?"

"It's nothing," he told her. "Some glass."

"Then it went well for you, too?"

"Well enough. I'm still alive."

There followed a few safe days of elation when Hans

could go to class feeling freedom, like pure helium, all about him. Those were the good days, the nights of sound sleep; but all too soon his conscience and Sophie's prodding brought the first agonized dabblings with another leaflet.

"Do you think it'll last a long time?" he had said to her. "I mean, statistically speaking, it can't last forever."

"What can't?" she had replied. Hans couldn't imagine her mind focusing on anything else.

"Us. What we're doing," he said irritably.

"Hans, we mustn't worry about the end right at the beginning."

She was so sure. Her certainty frightened him, but in those days fear was in the air he breathed.

A shrill, inhuman scream snapped Hans back to the prison cell.

"Sophie, they're hurting you!"

But the cry came again, and he knew this time it belonged to a man. It could easily become his own, when the interrogators returned. They had been absent two hours, and waiting was a kind of torture. He dared not relax. He must guard against his own weakness.

"I can't lose my nerve," he told himself. Imprisonment, torture, possibly even death awaited him, but he must protect the others. The lives of many people depended on his resistance. He must juggle with calm nerves. Leaning forward, he tried to pray, but not for his daily bread. He would no longer ask that his trespasses be forgiven. Slowly his lips moved, but they formed no coherent words. If God's name was dead on his tongue, he would address himself. "You are the only one responsible," he said. "You must not fail them. Take all the punishment upon yourself." He began to tremble. He felt weak and small. "O God," he whispered. "Give me death before I harm them." This was foolishly melodramatic even to his own ears. But his mind was made up. When his interrogators returned, he would give a full statement. He would say that the entire plot was his, that no others were involved.

The slender interrogator returned before dusk. He stood silently as Hans delivered his prepared admission. His smile was subtle. "How odd. You and your sister must be telepathic. She said the same thing, almost word for word, about herself. She advised us, very appealingly, that you should be released."

"She's lying."

"Of course she is, my boy. We know very well you had accomplices."

"No! There were just the two of us."

"Scholl, you mean to say we have brought Christl Probst all the way from Innsbruck for nothing? It's pathetic the way he weeps, the way he keeps asking for a priest. He doesn't strike me as the sort who would falsely claim authorship of that nasty mess we found in your mouth. Now, now, don't pout. Your room was a great help, you know. That clever wastebasket of yours! And of course we have other resources. We know, for instance, about your connections with a fanatical professor at the University, a Professor Huber by name, and another medical student, Alex Schmorell. I suppose they have run away, as Probst tried to. Don't you think so? Wouldn't you like to tell us where?" Hans sat in stony

24

silence, as numb as if struck by a stone in the back of the head.

"Very well, sulk. We will find them ourselves. We have an idea about Alex Schmorell. He was last seen all rigged out in mountain-climbing gear. That will be fun for the dogs. So you can relax, dear boy. We may have a few more chats; but rest assured, you have provided all the information we need."

# CHAPTER TWO

● It was night again. A tin tray of food sat unwanted on the floor of the cell, and though Hans had not eaten for two days, he could not touch it. At first he had hoped for release, for Sophie at least. Now even the bitter consolation of self-sacrifice had been denied him. Let them starve him to death, chain him to a rock like Prometheus; no torment could equal the knowledge that he had brought down his friends, his sister.

Hans wondered if this ancient cell, smelling of mold and mice, had been preordained for him before he was born, had waited patiently as he played with tin soldiers, rode his first horse, saw his first black swastika. Perhaps that was so for all of them. Surely he had always thought of Christl as having a destiny. Morose, dogged, coolly stubborn, Christl appeared to have the makings of a martyr. There had always been a distance in him, a *noli me tangere* reserve that allowed for respect, even admiration, but never intimacy. As a prospective doctor, there had been many jokes about his lack of a bedside manner. Recently, for his wife's sake, he had taken up the study of Catholicism. But what was hardest of all to understand about Christl was that he, the solitary, the almost mystic, should be the only one of them who was married, the only one to experience the human range of love and tenderness.

While Christl was ascetic, withdrawn, and unfathomable, Alex Schmorell was outgoing and forthright. A careless, eager-looking fellow, tall and thin, Alex had a face shaped like a spade; you could dig ditches with him. Hans had met him when they were both members of the riding club at Komstat. Neither had enjoyed the Prussian atmosphere, the clicking of heels, but their friendship had survived the club. Except for their love of horses and their interest in medicine, they had seemed at first to have little in common. Where Hans was serious and intense, Alex seemed nonchalant, devil-may-care. He enjoyed a fencing match in the misty dawn like one of Tolstoy's hussars. He would jump a horse where no sane rider should, and talked of fast racing cars and of climbing Mount Everest. His fondest dream was of sailing alone around the world in a small boat. It wasn't the danger that held him back, it was the lack of an audience.

"One day you'll get yourself killed for no good reason. I suppose you know that," Hans had said.

"Of course, one day, but in the meantime . . . Hans, I mean this. I believe the moment of birth is when we first know about death. Certainly you can't savor one without being conscious of the other. Death helps us know

28

what's worthwhile in life, what's rubbish." Alex could speak with a kind of relish of his dying. "I want to die like a lonely old animal, the last of a species, high among rocks and pitiless nature. No huddling nurses, no tearful relatives, no boot-licking morticians."

Death was a hateful thought to Hans, a wall. He never spoke of it, tried not to think of it, and kept Alex from the subject when he could. Usually, the best way to avert this disturbing topic was by music and song, for here the two had really found one another. Alex's voice was wailing and toneless as a muezzin's, while Hans intoned through his nose. "You know, Scholl," Alex admonished him, "you really ought to have those adenoids out." But singing together, they had something. "A gestalt! We are absolutely a genuine gestalt!" Alex had declared, and from then on they would render anything in duet from "The Lorelei" to Brahms's "Lullaby." Even the "International" or "The Horst Wessel Song," with Alex providing vigorous accompaniment on his balalaika, was better than silence. Alex knew his instrument. He used to play it at weddings for a fee of twenty marks. He had made quite a bit of petty cash that way, until the balalaika was classified as non-Aryan, and he was forbidden to play it.

Their common interest in medicine had brought the three young men to inspect Munich University in the autumn of 1938. On the last evening of their visit, a drooping canopy of clouds hung over the city. Was it fate that drew them out into a night that threatened rain, drew their feet along toward the misty glare of thousands of bare electric bulbs? The evening rang, thumped,

**29**

clashed, and squealed with Oktoberfest, Munich's October Festival. They paced the fringe, still clinging to darkness and silence.

"I wonder how medical school will be," Christl remarked.

Alex walked with his head down, shoulders wagging, a performing bear. "Lovely, if Herr Adolf doesn't turn the world into a cream puff and swallow it before we have a chance to find out."

Less than a year before, Germany had joined in a pact with Italy and Japan. In March, General Guderian had used a Baedecker guidebook to lead German panzer divisions into Austria, to save that country from political chaos. Now it was Czechoslovakia's Sudetenland, and Chamberlain had traveled in Hitler's bombproof train to Berchtesgaden.

It was already raining in the mountains. In Munich, the air was heavy with moisture, and the smoke from dozens of grill fires was held close to the ground. Everyone talked of war, and acted as though this were a last holiday.

Hans, remembering it all, could recall no inkling, as they strolled on the fringe of the crowd, that the evening was in any way special, that before it was over something would happen that would leave them more than friends.

Bavarian bands, roller coasters, beer-hall tents and half-drunken crowds packed the Theresienwiese during the century-old festival, and the three friends had held back from it like swimmers about to be plunged into strange waters. Christl drew hard on his pipe. A silent sort, talking only when excited, he was quiet now. Hans had learned to recognize his moods, and he had seen Christl through worse ones.

There was no apparent explanation for them. "Does gloom just come on like a fog inside you, darkening your windows?" he had asked, and Christl had looked startled. "Of course! That's exactly the way it is. How on earth did you guess?"

"We'll dedicate the evening to cheering you up," Alex had said.

"Frankly, I'd as soon go home to bed."

"First let's try a carousel. That ought to brighten your windows."

Had fate had a hand even in that, in choosing that particular carousel, in placing a Jew there on a white horse with red polka dots, a place where no Jew in his right mind should be? A small, fragile Jew with a thin, passionate face.

With a clang, the carousel began its slow revolutions along with the first steamy gusts of music. Around they went, sandwiched between uniformed Hitler Youths—the girls, Jungmadels, with slim legs in heavy shoes, and the boys, young Pimpfe, with great gnawed pretzels garlanded about their necks. Faster and faster . . . red and yellow lights blurring into comets . . . and whirling somewhere in the spectrum, a six-pointed star. Hans could not believe it. A Jew, here in public, right down to the telltale pariah's patch of yellow on his coat. Two Hitler Youths left their seats in a gaudily painted swan and moved up behind him while the music shrilled and the horses rode high and low. No voice could be heard above the din of the calliope. Hans waved a frantic warning as the two young men came on grinning, hand over hand.

31

The white polka-dotted horse ducked low. Hans could not seen it for a moment, and when it rose again the seat was empty; empty without a cry. The Jew must have been flung off onto the ground somewhere, but the carousel was moving too fast, and everything was blurred.

Hans and his companions alighted before the rotation had entirely stopped. There was the victim, mud-spattered, blood oozing from his lip.

"You'd better get out of here. Quick—I mean it," Alex urged him, but the Jew seemed dazed. "Come along. I'll give you a hand." Christl took him by the other shoulder, while across the turning arch of the carousel the Hitler Youths gazed with languid interest.

"We'd better vanish before they get after us," Hans urged. "Let's lose ourselves in that flea circus."

"As performers?" asked Alex.

Six of the Youths, fingers hooked in their belts, sallied indifferently after them.

Alex stopped at a shooting gallery and took out some coins.

"This is a hell of a place to start trouble," Hans protested. Christl, too, urged Alex along. The Hitler Youths had halted three booths away, where they were throwing darts at a target representing the Wandering Jew.

"What's your name?" Alex asked their new companion.

"Saul."

"That's a warrior's name. Did you come here looking for a fight?" Saul only shrugged. He seemed in no hurry to move along. "You know you'll lose."

"I'll give some hurt in return," Saul replied. "They

took my parents yesterday. My home is boarded up. I don't care what happens to me."

"Well, you're on our conscience till we get you out of here. And look, Saul . . . get rid of that star." But the Jew seemed to regard the pariah patch as a badge of honor. Almost forcibly they reversed his overcoat. "Now maybe we can disappear. Let's get out of here. Come on, Alex, move!" Alex seemed ready as usual for trouble, but Hans led him toward a beer tent.

"Cowards!" Alex condemned them all. "You quite evidently don't follow the famous maxim, 'Act so that every one of your actions may become a universal law.' "

"Rotten nonsense."

"Well, it was Kant who said it."

"It's still rotten nonsense."

The Hitler Youths, their number now increased to eight, followed slowly, prolonging the fun, perhaps awaiting the darker shadows that adhered to any path leading from the bright fairgrounds.

Hans and Christl marched their two reluctant companions down the main avenue of brewery tents: Löwenbräu, Augustinerbräu, Bäckerbräu, Hofbräu, and many others. Beer fumes hung in the air like fog. "I wish we had some girls along," Alex said. "Hans, why isn't Sophie here? Your sister's a lovely girl, and someone ought to tell her so."

"Hurry up," Hans urged him on. "We don't want to be caught in any dark corners."

"Lord, they're still after us," Christl whispered. "More of them." and he began to trot until all four pushed inside the Löwenbräu tent, into the crowd, the smoke, the noise. Before they could find a table, the Hitler Youths shoved by the doorman. Now they were ten.

The beer hall tent was packed with men and women, the majority as red with gulped beer and as grotesquely patriotic as the swastika draped walls. Under the interrogatory glare of carriage-wheel candelabra a lederhosen brass band thundered. Sweating patrons banged liter steins of beer in fierce time.

"A fine place for a Jew," Saul whispered, but he looked oddly amused, even triumphant. "Too bad Hitler's not here. I've something special for him."

When Alex had been forcibly seated at a long wooden table, Hans signaled to one of the plump waitresses in dirnall dress. She sailed toward them balancing a tray, of ten liter steins, which she set down with a crash.

*"Schatzl!"* she cried. "What can I get for you nice fellows?"

*"Ein Grosses,"* said Alex. "A big one. I want to drown myself."

Hans's plan, as much as he had formulated one, was to appear settled down for a long evening and, once the Hitler Youths relaxed their guard, to bolt and vanish. He spoke to the others. Christl was receptive, Saul noncommital, but Alex affected a debonair manner that worried him.

At other tables people were swaying, arms linked, in time to the music. A ponderous *gemütlichkeit* joined students in college hats with pear-shaped, bullnecked burghers. "Won't it be fine," mused Alex, "when all the unfit and the undesirable and the old have been put away?" He spoke in singsong and accompanied himself on the table with the heel of his hand in imitation of a

34

tribal drum. "Here comes the dear radish lady. Look at her big, feathered hat!" Hans paid for four huge, rosetted white radishes covered with salt crystals that felt like pebbles in his mouth.

The Hitler Youths had settled not far away. A group of girls had joined them, and the boys seemed absorbed in flirting. Hans did not look at them directly, but remained aware of them as a person in bed may be conscious of spiders in a far corner of the ceiling.

"Any minute now," he told the others.

Sounds collided, fell to the beer-dampened floor. Then, abruptly, an alarm knifed through the din, bringing instant silence and attention. Hans could hear the fans whispering in the high ceiling. The only thing that could have wrought such a change was a siren, followed by Hitler's voice ringing over the public-address system. From a confusion of memories and shadowy superstitions, the Führer fashioned clouds of glory and conquest, and his listeners breathed in the fumes. As an invocation for divine strength, a hoarse cry escaped from the amplifiers. His voice sobbed, words ran together as though he were about to recite in tongues: homeland, race, blood, soil, honor. For years Germany had patiently endured the wrongs inflicted by international Jewry. No more! . . . by Austrian decadence. No more! Now they were being asked to be patient again with the political opportunists of Czechoslovakia. How much more must Germany suffer?

"If he were only here in the flesh!" Saul's eyes were closed. He seemed to be thinking aloud. "Lord, give me a chance to get even!"

Hitler's voice filled the tent. The young Nazis, who

had risen, either to go outside or to create a scene, sat down again hastily, for when the Führer spoke, Germany listened. Those caught in public places heard him out or suffered the consequences: Gestapo interrogation, loss of job, or a back-alley beating by the SA. He spoke of peace and sounded like a hound of war. Gradually, the accumulated spittle of a lifetime filled Hitler's mouth. Soon, thought Hans, he will have the steins jumping.

"My God, my eardrums!" exclaimed Alex. "How long can he go on like that? What does he want from us now, an arm and a leg?"

Hans leaned toward his reckless friend and nodded in the direction of the Hitler Youths. They were all whispering with furious animation and casting glances in the direction of Alex and his friends. "Must you make a display of yourself, Alex? It's not a good idea for any of us."

"Pin-headed gladiators! Ant soldiers!" muttered Alex.

"No more out of you," pleaded Hans. "pretend you're patriotic. Try!"

"Damn it, I am patriotic!" Alex insisted loudly. "You think I'm drunk."

"Keep your voice down, that's all."

"I would if he'd shut that toilet seat of a mouth."

Others had taken notice. Smiles were few, and from the pack of Hitler Youths came only baleful, unwinking stares. They needed no further provocation, but Hitler's voice was a leash that held them back. "We'll be in for it soon," whispered Hans. "Our only chance is to bolt out of here while he's still ranting. Afterward it'll be too late."

"Suits me," said Alex.

Hans consulted the other two. It was fifty feet to

the side entrance, which was presided over by two cretinous bouncers who slumped sleepily on a bench to one side of the open tent flap. "Ready?" Hans whispered. "All right. Now! Run like hell!" The effect was electric. Alex raced for the exit, the others stampeding after him. Feet pounded behind them and a pair of barrel bodies lunged to catch them, but too late. The four of them were out in the street and sprinting. Not so the Hitler Youths, whose furious shouts followed them. Around the corner they ran and into the shadows, where they pulled up, panting hard.

"Damn it, Alex," Hans said. "If your idea is to get us into trouble, you're doing just fine."

Alex belched softly in the darkness. "They're cripples," he said. "They can't even run. Come on, Saul. Let's get out of this place."

Loudspeakers whirred around them. From the crackling static the speaker's voice leaped out, as sharp and vicious as a dogfight. All else was silence. The woman at the sausage stand rested her chin on the thick white pillars of her arms. She listened intently, her mouth wide open, one gold tooth gleaming. Thousands of river fish roasted in pits and were not eaten. Thousands of pretzels went unsold. The rollercoasters and the rifle ranges were still, the barker at the freak show was silent while the voice raved on and on.

"Have you eaten?" Hans asked.

"Don't worry about it," Saul replied.

"Have you a place?"

"I know a place."

"I mean a home," Hans persisted.

"We used to live in Schwabing, out near the University."

"And now?"

"What does it matter?"

They couldn't send him off like a stray dog. They couldn't adopt him, either, and it was only beginning to dawn on Hans why Saul was here at all. He was no moth drawn helplessly to the fatal Light. Clearly Saul was here deliberately seeking the fire.

The crowd began to thin. The lights dimmed, and the loudspeakers, which had been reverberating on every side, sounded far behind them.

"I hear feet running," whispered Christl. "I'm sure of it."

The four turned from the lighted street into a darker alley; an echo of feet and then silence; feet again, and a chain of figures like a silhouette of paper dolls linked itself across the alley's entrance. Before they could gain the other opening, it, too, was closed.

"Come on! Come on, you dirty swine!" Saul shouted. He had bent over a pile of trash in the alley and came up with a length of rusted metal in one hand.

"Well, I'm glad Sophie isn't here after all," commented Alex as the attack began. Alex, who could talk his way out of almost anything, raised both hands. "Peace!" he proclaimed. *"Pax vobiscum!"* But somebody grabbed him. The four feet scraped the ground as if their owners were performing a clumsy dance. Clinging together, the pair lurched into the wall. Alex tried bellowing a hymn. When this failed, he lashed out like a windmill with his long arms.

For a moment the fight was general: three against twelve.

Christl would not fight, but they beat him anyway.

Hans saw a sheath knife flash toward him, the little "blood and iron" dagger of the Hitler Youth. He snatched it away by the blade, never feeling the pain until later. When he flung it aside and hit out, the blood he saw on the other's face was his own. Then he was struck from behind and went down.

It wasn't valor that ended it, but the police, with whistles blowing and the clatter of booted feet. A single shot was fired, and at this the Hitler Youth retired. One, kicked by Alex where one ought never to be kicked, had to be carried. He was doubled over and screaming. Alex was the only one of them left standing, gasping and crying, but with the kick and one broken nose to his credit.

The police looked them over with a flashlight, muttered something about drunks and Oktoberfest and departed.

They had been lucky. Hans had lacerated fingers and a gash on his cheek and forehead. His face was swollen, his lips puffy, and the blood on his clothes was impressive. He had been frightened, but he was surprised that he had fought as well as he had.

"Hans, you need a slab of meat for that eye," Alex said. "You'll have a shiner tomorrow. Those pigs!"

"Did we hurt them any?" Hans asked, pulling out a handkerchief and trying to rub the blood off his jacket.

"You'll have to send it to the cleaners," Alex told him. "That handkerchief will do more good on your forehead. Do you feel all right, Hans?"

"I'm fine. Pull me up. I hope I made them bleed a little. Damn, my clothes are really a mess. How's Christl?"

39

"I hurt," said Christl, "but I'll live. Alex, why did you have to start this?"

"Well, it was interesting; you'll have to admit that," Alex replied.

It was then that they noticed Saul. He sat very still against the damp stone wall as if morosely considering the recent fight.

"Get up, Saul," Alex urged him.

His eyes were open, but he didn't move and he didn't breathe.

Alex took his hand, only to have the boy crumple over. "My God!"

It was after Alex had lit several matches that they saw it—a small black moth hole in the overcoat, a moth hole that had burned through the yellow star and into the boy's body. Saul was dead from the one shot that had been fired, that one warning shot from the police.

Hans sat under the bare, glaring bulb, which would burn in his cell all night. The Gestapo did not want its prisoners to kill themselves in the dark. The prison was quiet except for the occasional tread of the corridor guard, checking now and then at the various spy holes to see that all was well. The city above was silent too. The sky was overcast that night and the bombers could not get through. It was February, Friday the nineteenth, almost five years since the Jew named Saul had died.

Hans lay down on his sleeping mat. One end was rolled up to form a bolster for his head. Even if it had been comfortable, he could not have slept. It was too cold, and there was too much he still wanted to understand. Had it begun with the Jew? he wondered. No, not for him. For Alex, perhaps. A lot of gaiety had gone out of Alex that night.

They had left Saul's body where it lay. They could not bury him. They dared not mention it to the police, so they just went home.

"I killed him," Alex had said. "He paid the price of my clowning."

"They were after him before that, Alex. It wasn't your fault," Hans insisted.

"It was an accident," said Christl, by which he meant fate. And though it went unsaid in their discussions, it had occurred to Hans that it was a sort of suicide. No Jew in a normal state of mind would have gone to the Oktoberfest. Then it all went around in his head again. When you take a person's family and his home, leaving him with only the will to die, what else is it but murder?

"I don't know," Hans said aloud to himself. "I don't understand any of it." And there seemed so little time to figure it out, with snow dusting down the dark streets just before dawn.

# CHAPTER THREE

● Something had happened to their friendship after Saul's death. A casual camaraderie had become a dreadful sharing which precluded all others.

But for Hans, resistance had begun long before that. He had not known Christl or Alex when the Nazis first became real to him. That was on the day little Franz had appeared in uniform, and they had beaten him up and stoned the Bittner chickens.

Hans had only been an apple-crunching member of that summer bunch of boys. It was Otto who could hurl an apple into a tree and bring down harvests, Otto who could run faster, laugh louder, jump higher than any of the others. Hans remembered standing beside Otto on a warm and fragrant hillside. Solidly molded, Otto frowned upon the scene below. Heavy black brows, too heavy for his age, lowered across the bridge of his nose. Then he shouted at the small boy in the brown uniform driving a flock of chickens across the road.

"Hey, Ugly!"

Either the sound did not reach the boy in brown, or he pretended not to hear, though he began to drive the flock in the opposite direction. His carriage was upright, but one shoulder was higher than the other, as though, in the hands of a clumsy midwife, he had been born slightly crooked. He didn't seem to be running away. He was simply letting the chickens out into his father's field.

"Franz is so little. Let's leave him alone, Otto," said Hans.

Meditatively, Otto gnawed on a green apple. "You, Hans," he said. "Have another apple."

"They're not ours," objected Hans, but he held out his hand. Otto had spoken, and Otto was the leader.

Hans and the other boys followed Otto down the hill toward the gate where Franz stood, one shoulder raised, watching them.

"Hello, little Ugly," said Otto, and to the others, "Isn't he the ugliest thing you've ever seen?" In truth, Franz Bittner was a very unattractive child whose large translucent ears glowed incandescent in moments of stress. His hair was so pale as to be almost white, and his eyes a weak blue, so palely azure in their faded depths that Hans could not see into them. He looked to Hans as though he had been dipped in bleach so all the color had drained out of him, except for what the sun and embarrassment now brought into his face.

Then there was the brown uniform and the red arm band with its white circle and swastika.

"But Ugly certainly looks fine in his uniform," continued Otto. "Even a little knife, I see. And his father rides in a Mercedes. Why, Ugly's the most exceptional child in the world."

"Most exceptional! Most exceptional!" chorused some of the others.

"But I bet he hasn't cut his nails for a hundred years, or cleaned his ears." Franz stood his ground, but the blood looked ready to burst from his face. "That's because he doesn't know how. He can't do anything."

"He can't climb!"

"He can't swim!" They made a game of it, a competition of insults to a hapless victim. But Hans wondered if perhaps deep down Otto was jealous of the uniform and the Mercedes.

"I bet little Ugly knows how to wet his pants."

Franz kicked at the ground. As yet he hadn't said a word.

"Leave him alone," Hans urged.

"First," Otto persisted, "little Ugly's got to confess."

Franz squinted at his antagonist. In the sun, he could scarcely see.

"Confess the awfullest thing you ever did." Again Franz said nothing, so Otto confessed for him. "Ugly steals from his mother's purse. He cuts the tails off little dogs. Don't wet your pretty new uniform, Franz. We'll be going in a minute. Look at him! What a coward. His lip's all a-tremble."

"That's enough, Otto," insisted Hans, but the other paid no attention.

Otto swaggered closer and wagged one finger. "Be honest, little Ugly. You're a freak, aren't you? Answer yes or no." Franz was still silent. "I've heard that little

Ugly's most courageous. He goes around in cars with generals, you know. Now isn't that exceptional?" Otto directed a hissing laugh at the ground.

At last Franz spoke. "Please," he begged. "Please." He should have commanded, thought Hans. He should have ordered them out of his father's field.

Otto clicked his heels. "Is that an order, Field Marshall? Men, do you hear that?"

Again Franz did the wrong thing. He threw a stone at Otto's face, and missed. Otto laughed, but his face flushed and his ears seemed to move back like a greyhound's. "Well, if you take it like that . . ." Carefully he removed his cap and shoved it into his jacket pocket. Then he hung the jacket on the fence and advanced. For a moment Franz held him at bay by wildly cudgeling the air. Then Otto hit him hard, and Franz fell as though a chair had been pulled from under him. His mouth looked like a round red flower. Hans thought it was over, but the boy got up slowly, smiling, spitting and bleeding. It was horrible to see him rising so deliberately. He'll be killed, thought Hans, moving to intervene. For his trouble Hans received a stinging wallop in the chest. Franz shrieked while Hans grasped him in both arms, managing to imprison his puny fury and shielding him from further blows. The boy's body felt like a bony cage, frail but fatally single-purposed. Hans held him down with all his strength while Otto stood over them, feet spread, breathing hard.

"Well, that's it," he finally said.

"I hope that's it," said Hans. Anyone's violence upset him, his own most of all.

With Otto goading them, the others turned to the

46

chickens. Calling them "Ugly's army," the boys were searching for things to throw. Heady with imagined battle, they charged across the field, flinging apples and yelling with cannibal gee. "Yah - yah - yah . . ." Chickens scattered before them.

Franz's face was ashen. He had given up resisting, but his breathing cut like a saw. That worried Hans. He had heard that Franz had asthma attacks. It all seemed so rotten. He didn't like what was going on, but he didn't like Franz, either. It was hard to like a person who looked as though he had been raised on fish food, with watery eyes and a mouth like an incipient blister. Hans tried not to look at him. He could hear the others cheering, and now Franz began to blubber unashamedly, spinning threads of pink saliva. "O God, God," wept the boy. God's name only made Hans feel worse. Not that he expected divine intervention, but God was a very large thought.

"Listen, Franz, don't cry. I'll let you go. Come on, get up."

"You'll hear from my father about this! You will!" The voice was wispy, without malice. "They're killing the chickens, Hans!" The last was a desperate appeal.

"I can't stop them. Where's your father, Franz?"

Across the field the boys had crowded the flock into a tight corner of the fence. Beneath their shouts Hans could hear the repetitious croaking of creatures in pain. "They're torturing them, Hans!"

"All right. All right. We'll try."

Even as Hans approached, the uproar ceased. A girl, small but sturdy, with heavy dark-brown hair which gave her an air of assurance, stood between the boys and their prey. There was a chicken cradled in her arms. "Go on, throw them at me!" she shouted.

Embarrassed by his own excesses or actually intimidated by the girl's kindling eyes, Otto was in grudging retreat.

"Hans!" she shouted, ignoring the others. "Come and help! These poor creatures . . . this one's leg is broken."

"Sophie, you shouldn't be here. You'll get hurt," Hans admonished his younger sister.

"It's these chickens that are hurt. The poor things."

Franz rounded up his flock, more ruffled than damaged by final count, except for the one Sophie held. "Franz," she asked, "may I take her home? Hans can make a splint for her leg, and I'll look after her." The boy nodded, very close to tears again. "It's all right now, Franz. It's all over."

Hans and his sister started for home. Sophie carried the injured hen. They talked little. When she said, "Poor little Franz," just to start a conversation, Hans replied bitterly because he had not done more. "He's a zero, Sophie, and you know it."

"I know, but still . . ."

"He told me the other day he once saw Jesus in a ball of light under his bed." Hans remembered how hard it had been to keep a straight face when Franz had told him this, but Sophie only said, "Really? I wish I had seen Him, too."

Once home, Hans made the splint and helped Sophie build a nest in the ramshackle tool shed, which had become a hospital for injured and abandoned creatures, wild and tame. Some died there and were duly buried, but many recovered, thanks to or in spite of Sophie's ministrations.

The episode might have ended in the shed, had not Franz's father arrived that night. Herr Bittner was short, but as thickly set as a stevedore. Hans's father had responded to his heavy knock and opened the door, peering out into darkness through reading glasses that had slipped to the end of his nose. "Yes, please?" he said to the uniformed silhouette. "Won't you come in? It's a cold, wet night." He stood aside in his carpet slippers, one long finger marking the place in his book, as the booted figure strode in and stood at attention.

"Herr Bittner. What a surprise. If we're about to be sociable, I wonder if you would mind . . . those wet boots of yours . . . do sit down, Herr Bittner. Please."

"I'm sorry, Herr Scholl; these boots are practically a part of me." His voice was loud and volleying. "They've seen me through a good many street battles with fanatics in this country."

"And I'm sure you've made good use of them. Please, Herr Bittner, have a chair. Have a schnapps."

The visitor took schnapps only. The glass in his hand, he continuously paced, fondly enumerating his scars: the one across his upper lip, another across the lower jaw, the many which his uniform concealed, and finally the monument revealed by his limp. He had received that during the early days of the movement, in direct physical defense of his leader.

"Surely, Herr Bittner, you didn't come out in the rain to relate your medical history."

"Quite right, Herr Scholl. I am here expressly in behalf of myself and my son to express our gratitude to your children, Hans and Sophie." He went on to elaborate the affair with the chickens. "And how is the little nurse doing with her hen?"

"It's recovering, or so Sophie tells me. Herr Bittner, what is it I can do for you?"

"Hear me out, Herr Scholl. Your children are good German material. As you know, I possess a certain status in our movement. I could get your son handsomely launched in our youth program. Your daughter, too. Perhaps you have heard of our new German Girls' league. Sophie is just the right age to join the Jungmädel."

"I'm sure this is very kind."

"Yes, I can introduce them to important people in the movement, men who will soon be important in Germany and the world. Roehm, Himmler . . . all the leaders, in time."

"But surely, your leader . . . you cannot take him seriously?"

"Perhaps not. Roehm's a coarse man, a crude fellow. But Himmler! Now there's someone to watch. With your son in his SS legion, his future would be assured in the Germany of tomorrow."

"Actually, I was referring to Adolf Hitler."

"Herr Scholl! We do not joke about the Führer. Mind you, he will seize power in Germany one day."

"I'm surprised. Is there any power in our country to seize? I must confess, I find Hitler's speeches reassuring. What sensible person could take him seriously?"

Bittner attended this silently, but the veins stood out in his short neck and his face was flushed. "Herr Scholl jokes, yes? Of course. But Hitler's tide is coming in. Humor won't stop it. If one does not swim with the tide, one drowns, I assure you."

"But when the tide goes out, what then? The beach begins to stink, does it not?"

50

Herr Bittner all but clicked his heels. He looked like a man about to answer a call to arms. "Herr Scholl, I am sorry. I had hoped to give your son a rare opportunity. Perhaps you will one day think better of your attitude. If so, you know where to find me. Now, if our business is concluded, you will excuse me." He heaved himself toward the door and jerked it open without awaiting a reply.

"My good Herr Bittner. It's a cold night. Would you mind?" The door closed like a gunshot. "Ah," sighed Hans's father, turning the latch.

"Hans, did you hear all that?" Hans had appeared on the landing. "I thought I saw your shadow. Not a very nice practice, eavesdropping, but it does save words. I don't like that Bittner. I feel sorry for his son. Forced to march about in uniform, and being fed those Nazi ideas."

Hans said, "I don't know if it's any worse than being forced to remain outside the program. I mean, the offer was for me, Father, and you didn't bother to consult me. You didn't have to insult him."

"That awful man, Hans? Will you listen to me?" It did not occur to Hans to do otherwise, though he preferred his father during periods of neglect. "It takes care and love and time for a boy to grow to manhood. A boy needs rich soil to grow in. I'm not sure there's any of that soil left in Germany. Not enough of it, surely. And none of it is in that Nazi desert. Later you can make up your mind about these things, but trust in me now. And Hans . . . I was proud of you and Sophie today. The way you stood up to what was wrong. That took courage. You're too young to sense this, Hans, but there are a great many stunted souls who don't know what to do with their lives. That's why they want to change the world for everyone else."

During this statement his father had taken hold of Hans's hand, seeking some response there. Feeling none, he let the boy's hand slip away.

"May I go to my room, sir?"

"You may. But think about what I've said."

His father made one last attempt at comradeship. He tried to ruffle Hans's hair, but Hans avoided the gesture. He stared at the floor so as not to meet his father's eyes, for his father looked sad and suddenly old, and that made Hans feel scared and sick inside. Hans caught sight of himself in the mirror at the head of the stairs and called himself a name. He tiptoed on to his own room and saw himself again in the bureau mirror wearing an expression that puzzled him. He couldn't have said so to his father, could scarcely admit it to himself. But part of him, a very nearly controlling part, had yearned to join the others in throwing apples, as a part of him now yearned to wear a uniform and march in a stomping crowd that made older people get quickly out of the way. "Only a part of me," he told himself, but enough so that he felt irritated with himself and with his interfering father.

Hans lay down on his bed. Outside, the night was loud. Boom, boom, boom went a big drum, and torchlight flickered on the ceiling. He would hear all the details from a wild-eyed Franz tomorrow: how the "battle of the bands" had taken place in Ulm, and how it would be long remembered. "There were the Reichsbanner and the Storm Trooper band. You should have seen them.

52

You should have heard them trying to outplay each other. People were shouting and laughing, Hans, it was terrific! I wish you'd been there." But in the darker alleys, as Hans's father told it, the Storm Troopers had stalked with their spring-loaded steel pipes, cutting down any stray Reichsbanner man before he could shout *"Freiheit!"* ("Freedom!") It had not been amusing in the back streets of Ulm on that late August night in 1931, according to Herr Scholl, but even his report had a sinister attraction in it. It made Hans yearn to be a part of what was really happening in his country.

CHAPTER FOUR

● The seeds had been planted on the day of the chicken raid, but it was not until Hitler became Chancellor in January of 1933 that his father was forced to permit Hans's entry into Otto's troop of Hitler Youth. Never once did his father look at him in uniform, nor did he say good-bye on that early autumn morning of the same year when the troop was honored by an invitation to the Nazi Party Day of Victory at Nuremberg.

Hans took his guitar, a book, and the folded banner. He was troop flag bearer, an honor all his own. Only Sophie walked with him to the train. She wore the Jungmädel uniform: clomping shoes, blue skirt, white blouse, and cotton neckerchief held by a wooden ring that bore the group insignia. She looked well in her uniform, but according to her troop leader, a young woman put together like Egyptian sculpture, Sophie did not mix easily. She lacked enthusiasm, and stumbled while marching. Her eyes were tested, but no glasses were prescribed. Sophie was a sleepwalker in broad daylight, which hardly conformed to the eagle-eyed outlook expected of German youth.

"Why does Father hate me so?" Hans had asked her as they walked to the station.

"Hate you, Hans? That's an awful thing to say. He loves you."

"Well, he certainly seems to get love and hate mixed up."

Maybe it wasn't hate, but, whatever it was, their communications had become brief, formal, and punctuated solely by question marks and exclamation points.

Hans and Sophie hadn't gone far when Franz joined them. Half tadpole, half frog, he had grown less than the others. He was a plump, flap-eared, unhappy boy who had found vulgarity the easiest way to acceptability. Because of the occasion and his father's close association with Ernst Roehm, they greeted him with a display of enthusiasm. Hans even contrived to slap him on the back. Comrades!

"Have you brought the flag?" Franz asked excitedly.

"Here it is, all rolled up."

"I mean the special troop flag."

"Under my coat," Hans told him.

"It was nice of you to make it, Sophie," Franz said.

The flag, which was yellow and bore a green griffin, was to be unveiled as a surprise for the rest of the boys. It would be a unique troop banner. Franz, who had designed it, hoped to be its bearer.

The station was packed when they arrived. Various troops were loading, mingling, getting lost. Otto Braun, their troop leader, was shouting angrily at his straggling charges, a process that made his pustular face even redder. Not games, but a street brawl, had broken his nose. "He's a fighter," Hans had said of him with admiration, but Herr Scholl called him a gutter cat.

Gutter cat or hero, Otto led them in all things, in target practice on the churchyard monuments as readily as in football. Throughout a game, Otto would praise, blame, appeal to their sentiments, lead charge after headlong charge. Usually his team won, but if they lost, Otto would limp off the field, savage tears rolling down his cheeks. It was action, not words, with Otto. Take the business with their teacher. They had all been amused by his frequent references to "the good old days," and his habit of greeting his class with a stiff little bow and "What has Herr Schicklgruber in store for us today, I wonder?" Hans had often laughed, though he knew such a man was headed for trouble. It had taken Otto to draw up a statement. The next day there had been an assembly, with the teacher standing stiff and very pale before a slow procession of Brownshirts who took their turn spitting on him. That was going a bit far, Hans had to admit, though he didn't say so to his father. When Herr Scholl spoke of a man's right to listen to a different drummer, Hans had told him, "Musical taste is apt to change. I believe I heard that teacher joined the Party and was reinstated." He had heard no such thing.

"Scholl!" Otto was shouting. "Scholl, what the hell are you doing? We're all aboard. And what's that damned thing—a guitar? You can't take that. Give it to your sister." Hans protested. "Not one word, Scholl. That's an order!"

All the way to Nuremberg, Hans rode beside Franz,

who talked about the banner and the ceremony of its unveiling. At that moment Franz Bittner would become somebody, or so it seemed to Franz.

From the Nuremberg yards, Otto made them kick-step all the way to the Zeppelinwiese encampment. Except for the sight of Franz hopping like a cat in a puddle to keep in step, it was agonizing, and they were all exhausted when they arrived in the open field where a tent city had arisen. With four hundred cots in each vast tent, sixty thousand youths were housed there. Over a hundred thousand SA men and party officials were located in mass quarters around the city. One thousand doctors and twelve hundred nurses waited in attendance. The tumult, the glitter, the human and mechanical thunder of the Nazi Party Congress rose to the stars.

Otto read out the camp regulations: obedience to order, cleanliness, no walking in the woods, no swimming in the camp rivers, no carrying of daggers. When he dismissed his troop, only enough time and energy remained to eat supper and go to bed. Hans sat between Otto and Franz, and listened disconsolately to the sound of soup being sucked down, ten thousand bowls of it at once. Only Otto talked occasionally, made a joke or two. "Hans thought this'd be like the children's festival at Dinklsbühl. All lollypops and pink balloons." *Isn't Hans a fool?* Though the last sentence was left unsaid, Hans knew it was implied. Somewhere a radio played loudly, a special program called "The Big Sound from Nuremberg."

Assigned to a cot at last, Hans lay down, shivering from an ice-cold shower, and tried to read. "Scholl, what's that trash?" It was Otto again. "Give me that,

Zweig, . . . *Starry Hours of Humanity*. For the love of heaven, Scholl, you can't read this." He pocketed the book. "I think you want to get this troop into trouble. What if I began reading Freud or Einstein? My God, Scholl, you ought to know something about loyalty by this time." He prowled down the long rows of cots, each cot occupied by a rigidly prone boy waiting for the lights to go out. Presently the room was darkened. The blood beat inside Hans's head, and for a long time he was unable to sleep: four hundred boys, and not a single sound.

Next morning Hans bore the Party flag proudly: white for nationalism, red for the social idea of movement, and the black swastika for the struggle to victory of the Aryan man. Otto ordered them to sing, and they sang.

Our flag flutters ahead of us,
Into the future we march through night and death.

Troop after troop flowed into the great stadium and stood breathless before the high rostrum, waiting for their leader to appear. He was heralded by a whisper like a sea breeze passing over the ranks. He was not as tall as Hans had expected; short, really, with the build of a clerk who had sat out his life on high stools, but a clerk with eyes of fire. For a long time Hitler surveyed them in silence. He opened his clenched jaws, but no words came. He appeared to be paralyzed. Then, with a twist of his mouth as if his tongue were swollen, a hoarse shout escaped him. "My children . . ." echoed from the loudspeakers. Many shouted back, "Father . . . Father." He seemed overcome; his jaws worked, and slowly there

59

came a change, as though an electric charge had begun to flow through his body. Panting, he began to speak. Hans found the process terrifying. From one megaphone after another words rocketed back and forth in a voice that could demolish crystal goblets. His force and fury flowed into the stadium. At times Hitler closed his eyes, letting the river of sound flow unhindered. He jerked his head back until light sparked from his molars. His voice rose and fell, trembled, pleaded, snapped suddenly out like machine-gun fire, but for Hans something was terribly lacking. It came to him as a shock that the voice contained no human quality. It was as if an eagle in the mountain fastnesses, having found its eggs broken and its mate dead, had at last accomplished human speech. Hans became exhausted and depressed, but the voice played on, a full orchestra of sounds without one note of music. Far off, and faintly on another day in autumn, he seemed to hear his father talking, wistfully. "Things change. I can't enjoy seeing my children grow older, drifting away into a world I don't understand. I can't rush to the window anymore when I hear a parade. I can't turn on the radio and find decent music. I can't even fish with this river all filled up with trash from the new factory. Thank God we can still enjoy the seasons rolling by. What a lovely light this afternoon, Hans. Just look there in the trees."

Hitler vanished as quickly as he had come. Hans was scarcely aware of it except for the well-rehearsed outcry. "We want our leader . . . leader . . . leader!" barked the loudspeakers. "Nothing for us . . . everything for Germany." Hans opened his mouth with the others, but no sound came. "For Hitler we live . . . for

Hitler we die. Hitler is our Lord . . . who rules a brave new world." Blood pounded in his ears, and he yearned for solitude and time to think; time to walk in the autumn hills; time to hear the dropping of autumn apples, first one, then three or four at a time, until the ripe apples fell like rain. Hans imagined himself the last apple on the tree, wind-worked and finally plummeting through leopard-speckled autumn days.

He took a jolting step forward to catch himself from falling. Otto shot him a glance of irritation, eyes like daggers. Then they were singing again as troop after troop began to march stiffly away. Hans was hardly conscious of his surroundings, of the flag that tugged at his arms. He kept seeing himself in the wildly radiant faces of the others. "Do I look like that?" he kept asking himself, and then, "What has happened to me?" Had this estrangement been growing in him, or was it something born suddenly? Had he looked too close when his eyes should have been glazed?

He was given no chance to ponder, for Otto shouted at him, "You, Scholl! Are you all right? You almost dropped the flag." Hans wasn't the only one upbraided. They had all been slack, Otto informed them, glaring hard at Hans, and they would drill and drill until dusk. Then they would be assigned a campfire site in the hills, and when they went there, they would march in double time.

And they did march, smartly, into the raucous night that swelled about them with the deepening rumble of converging processions and the rosy light of torches. On a bare hillside they stopped to gather wood. Somewhere the Führer was speaking, and at a climactic moment

61

the signal to ignite fires would be given. When their pile was high enough, Otto ordered them into a circle around it. Time passed. Hans shivered from the cold. Then finally searchlights gracefully converged over the distant stadium where Hitler spoke. Shouts went up. Otto plunged in his torch, and for winking miles around, conflagrations were kindled.

A straw-stuffed, tar-smeared effigy, its hair and beard made from a mop, was produced by Otto and held aloft. "Here we have a typical Jew. Is he handsome?"

"No!" came the chorus. "Ugly!"

"Is he any use to Germany?"

"No!"

"What shall we do with him, then? Shall we let him go?"

"No. Burn him. Burn the Jew!"

So the dummy went into the flames, and smoke roared blackly up from the tar. The boys joined hands and formed a ring around the fire. Hans, watching them through half-closed eyes, seemed again to hear his father's voice murmuring inside his brain. "Germany's a strange land. No better poets or musicians, the most dedicated scientists and explorers, and then along come the Nazis." "They've done some good," Hans had objected. "They've given people jobs, and stopped the riots." His father replied, "And burned the books and opened the concentration camps." Hans had refused to believe that Hitler knew about the camps. "How could he help but know?" Hans had bitten his lips in furious disbelief. He found himself biting them now as the others began a circling movement that at first was awkward and dragging, but which gradually became more effortless, free

62

and rapid. As Otto watched approvingly, hands on hips, they whirled in earnest, throwing out monstrous shadows across the stony hillside.

Hans and Franz did not dance. Otto shook his head and walked toward them. "Scholl, I thought this was your sort of thing. Self-expression." But he gave no order, and when the pair failed to respond, he walked away to the fire, took a book from his pocket, and tore it slowly in half. Then he tore the halves into quarters and threw the scraps onto the fire. One book. Hans seemed to see them burning by thousands, a flame that licked the stars.

"When Jews were in the desert land," sang the throng of boys, "They chewed their garlic in the sand."

"My father once burned a book of mine," Franz said. "Bible stories with colored pictures. Did I tell you once how I had a vision?"

"Yes. Jesus under the bed."

"That's right." Franz sounded embarrassed. "Well," he continued, not looking at Hans, "he wanted me to say it was a lie. Like a little jackass, I ran off and he couldn't catch me. He has a bad leg, you know, but he burned the book where I could see him, and after I'd gone to sleep, he woke me up and tied me to a bed post. Then he used the strap."

"So you said it was a lie."

"Not at first. But he convinced me all right. That strap did."

"You must hate him."

"I deserved it. He's a great man." Between his father and God, Franz made little distinction. Both carried a punishing strap, and neither left room for a fluttering Jesus.

"I'd hate him all the same," said Hans.

The other boys chanted around the fire. "When they found there was a drought, Moses belched and the water came out." No longer did they hold hands. They thrust their arms into the air and yelled, howled, leaped and spun in boisterous devotion to the flames.

Franz peered unblinkingly at the performance. The fire must have hurt his weak eyes, but he did not turn from it. "We'll show him tomorrow, when we march with the new flag. Wait till they see me with that flag. . . . It was good of your sister to make it, Hans. So beautiful."

"Yes, it's a good job," Hans agreed.

"I mean your sister . . . Sophie."

Hans felt a sudden revulsion that this unlovely specimen of a boy should admire Sophie, though he was right. Not beautiful, perhaps, but lovely. It was perpetual autumn whenever Hans pictured her, with the yellow leaves sailing down, and Sophie gathering nuts and the last greens for her creatures. She gathered autumn flowers, too, but with everything else, by the time she got them home they were always crushed.

A convulsion of Franz's body brought Hans back to the firelight and the raging throng. Franz had lurched forward as though he might suddenly be sick, but instead he rose unsteadily. He was seized by a tremor that seemed about to wrestle him to the ground, then, without a backward glance or a word to Hans, he moved off toward the leaping crowd. Immediately the whirling circle absorbed him. There was no longer any singing, only weird shrieks, tongue noises, croaking sounds. It was like nothing Hans had ever heard before, primeval and frightening. Though the distance from him to the moving

64

figures was little more than that of an outstretched arm, the dancers seemed separated from him by a hundred thousand years. They chanted of things forgotten, of things which seemed to be a part of neither speech nor reason. Words seemed to assail, to enter him. "He calls you down, he calls you forth, beyond the dead, beyond the raised hands." There was Franz, pitching forward and back, jerked by a vitality beyond the tolerance of bone and muscle. And Hans discovered with horror that his own hand was beating time on the bare ground; his own hand, his body, wanted to join without his permission. Blindly he stumbled away. No one saw him depart. Halfway down the hill, a labor service team was pulling up loudspeaker cables to make way for a morning review. He did not look back. He dared not. For what if he saw in the blackness above the flames a shape with horns and wings?

Returning to the troop tent, Hans fell asleep almost immediately. He knew nothing of what had happened until he awoke in the half-dark of early dawn with Otto shaking him by the shoulder.

"Have you seen Franz?" Otto asked in a hissing whisper. He sounded worried, not angry.

"No."

"You didn't see him burned? Hell, he was pushed, or he fell. Personally, I think it was his own clumsiness. Anyway, he landed right in the fire. Squirmed all over the ground, his clothes on fire. It was horrible, really. And then he ran off. We couldn't find him in the dark. You've got to help me, Hans, before this gets out and messes up our record. Now, Scholl! Hurry, and I'll overlook your own peculiar behavior."

Hans would have gone in any case.

A misty dawn smelling of rain lay on the low hills where the fires still smouldered. They heard Franz before they saw him. He was groaning. "Are you all right, Franz?" Hans knelt beside him. The boy's eyes looked wet and naked, as if they had been peeled, and he smelled like a barbecue. "Franz, can you roll over? Let me see your back." Hans helped him move. "O my God, Otto. Look . . ." Great holes had burned completely through his clothes, and where the flesh was bare, blisters had risen, round and yellow as raw egg yolks. "Otto, help me get him to the medics."

"We don't need the medics. You'll be fine, won't you, Franz?" Otto addressed him heartily, and then in a whisper said to Hans, "For God's sake, Scholl! What did I tell you about keeping this quiet?"

Half walking, half being dragged between them, Franz was escorted to the troop tent. "You're doing fine, old man. Just fine. Hans, go get our courageous friend a cold drink. That'll fix you up, Bittner." Franz gave answer only with his eyes, and it was an appeal.

"He needs a doctor," insisted Hans.

"The flag," whispered Franz.

"Do you think he's delirious?" Otto looked worried.

Hans explained about the special troop flag. "Franz, you can carry it when we get home. That'll be all right, won't it?

"Sure, of course," said Otto.

Franz had closed his eyes. Every now and then he shivered as though he had been plugged into an electric socket, and Hans held him so that he would not vibrate right off the cot. In the end Otto decided to get a doctor.

66

To calm his own nerves, Hans talked about going home, about the troop flag and how it would look. Franz managed to pull the flag from beneath his pillow, and Hans promised to carry it. He couldn't manage two flags, but he would see that Franz's banner was in the parade.

"Thank you, Hans. Thank you for everything." After that Franz said not a word. Not a muscle moved in his face. If it hadn't been for the regular spasms of shivering, Hans might have thought he was watching a corpse.

A crowd of curious boys had gathered around the cot. They speculated about whether Franz would die. Bets were taken. Then they all fell silent as Otto arrived with two stretcher-bearers. After their departure, Otto lashed into them all, his voice like a jackdaw's, mocking and pecking. What were they standing around for? Didn't they know it was the last and most important day, the day of the big march?

The Storm Troopers had begun assembling as early as 3 A.M. for the consecration of flags on the Luitpoldhain. The Youth groups were not to be called upon until afternoon for the review and the final procession through the city center. Marching twelve abreast, it would take five hours for them all to pass the reviewing stands. Hans had delegated the new troop flag to Achim Becker, an unpopular boy not unlike Franz, who was nervously grateful for the honor. They were all lined up, shoulders back, stomachs in, ready to step off, when it happened.

Otto was passing down the line, reviewing his troop, when he saw the new flag. He stopped as though he were staring at a six-legged dog that had just crossed his path. "Becker, what is that?" He raised his upper lip in a smile that revealed big-square teeth. "Is that a griffin or a unicorn? Or is it your underdrawers? You know the regulations, Becker. Get rid of that laundry." Hans had never heard of the regulations, nor apparently had Achim. The small boy stood stiffly, still gripping the flagstaff. "Give it here, Becker. Give it here!"

Otto yanked the flag away as Hans stepped between them.

"Scholl, don't you ever keep your nose out of anything?" Two sharp creases had formed on either side of Otto's mouth. Hans made a fist. "Take hold of yourself, Scholl."

Slowly and painstakingly, Otto tore the flag in half. The sun's rays were blinding arrows probing for Hans's brain. With one hand he shielded his eyes from them. The other he drove with all his strength into Otto's stomach.

One furious instant; impulse without reflection, had made the difference. Yet it might all have happened anyway: Otto, dead at Stalingrad; he, Hans, in prison, and little Franz a worldly success now, a lieutenant in Hitler's elite bodyguard.

Certainly he could not have foreseen it then, riding back to Ulm in disgrace. Tired and subdued, the Ulm troop had boarded the train. Hans had spoken to no one, and no one spoke to him. He studied the yellow slip that had assigned him to a car, the red one that had furnished him a cot during the rally. He did not join in the sporadic singing or the recapitulations, nor did he speculate about Franz's fate or his own. When he saw Otto doubled over, he'd known part of his life had ended. He had been confined to the tent, finished for good with the Hitler Youth. Any prospects of making a Youth leader

68

or attending the Adolf Hitler School were finished, yet all he had felt was weary relief. All he wanted was a hillside strewn with autumn leaves, his feet sinking into that soft carpet, and mud oozing up between his toes. He wanted a handful of good Bavarian chestnuts that were always stacked beside the Bittner barn, and he wanted to startle his father with a few things. "Have you heard of Krupp's agricultural tractor scheme?" he might start out. "Well, it's not tractors they're building." He might begin that way, or he might tell his father about all the trains shunting back and forth in the Nuremberg yards. He'd let him know it was nothing but practice for moving troops in war.

The train rattled south. Most of the boys slept. Otto passed once down the aisle, but did not speak. Hans glanced at the Party newspaper, *Völkischer Beobachter*, which told how Hitler had closed the Congress with ringing statements on race purity and the failure of democracy. Then he closed his eyes, and did not awaken until the train pulled into the outskirts of Ulm. Far off, the town was visible. The Danube was polished silver. All was peaceful, and Hans's eyes fixed on a bit of yellow light that had transfixed the cathedral steeple. "How very beautiful," he told himself. How very beautiful it was.

# CHAPTER FIVE

● There was so much to sort out in his mind, Hans thought, sitting in his cell. He could hardly remember now why he had struck Otto that day in Nuremberg. It certainly wasn't over something worth dying for. He had admired Otto, had never really disliked him. Except for his exclusion from the Hitler Youth program, there had been no recrimination. He had simply lost touch with Otto until three months ago, when a letter, a sort of last testament, had arrived from Stalingrad. As much as the fight, perhaps, that letter had driven him on to the final act, which might cost him his life.

The ceiling light seemed to have lost power, for the daylight from the high window diffused it. Hans tried to look out of the window, but could only pull himself as high as a penciled legend: *You can't see anything but a brick wall. I've already tried it.*

He washed his face and hands at the small sink. There was neither hot water nor soap. Later, after a breakfast of ersatz coffee and bread, a man in civilian clothes arrived. He looked like a choir boy suddenly caught up by middle age. His cherubic cheeks were beginning to parch and his slicked hair partially concealed a glistening bald spot. He introduced himself cheerfully. "I hope we will become intimately acquainted in the next few days. I'm your attorney. And I must say I'm glad to find you in such good shape after the shock of your arrest. May I sit down?" Hans indicated the other plank cot. "Ah, that's better. I've had quite a morning. Quite exhausting. My son's birthday, and now this. I won't deceive you, Scholl. You're in a mess."

"I take it I have no choice of counsel," said Hans.

"Count yourself lucky," replied the attorney, looking around.

"You can tell them I haven't the slightest intention of committing suicide. Perhaps they'll turn off the light at night."

"I should hope not," said the lawyer, who seemed to be examining the contents of a package that Hans at first took to be a brief. "They have left out a piece," he said irritably. "And with toys so hard to get!" He showed Hans the toy he had purchased with difficulty for his son's birthday. It was broken.

"Will the trial be soon?" asked Hans. "There will be a trial?"

"I have no idea when it will be," said the lawyer. "Perhaps it would be a good idea if you'd disclose anything you think might be useful for your defense." His eyes roamed the walls as if examining them for inscriptions or signs. "I suppose I should know everything you did as well as the things you didn't do. Then I can decide what to do with you." Hans was silent. "Do say something. I'd rather like to get out of here and see if I can have this broken thing replaced."

"How do I know you're not here from the Gestapo?"

"You don't." The man spoke in a monotonous voice, as though reciting a multiplication table. "One way or another, I am your best hope."

"Could you tell me whether my parents have been informed of this . . . this business?"

"I presume they know. It was in the papers."

"Then they will attend the trial?"

"Do you want them there?"

"No, I don't." This was the last thing Hans wanted. He had caused them enough suffering.

"Well, that will be at the discretion of the court. It has nothing to do with you or me," said the advocate. "I must say you don't seem to appreciate the seriousness of your position."

"In this place? How can I fail to appreciate it? Please, how is my sister? Will they hurt her"

"I couldn't know."

"And Christl Probst?"

The lawyer only frowned over his briefcase. Putting on steel-rimmed glasses and unfolding a sheet of paper, he read from what purported to be an indictment for treason. "Is that perfectly clear? Would you like me to read any of it again?" he asked when he had finished.

"Yes, perfectly clear," whispered Hans. An invisible version of himself, smaller, curled up into a ball, was crying, "Please, someone save me."

"Will you kindly stop mumbling? It is against the rules, and besides . . . Look here, I came out of kindness."

"I know it! I know it!" said Hans convulsively. He had already put the man down as a Nazi informant.

The lawyer jerkily changed the position of his body and clasped his restless hands. "How does anyone sleep on this bed? No, no, keep attentive now. You have a perfectly good defense; one that may save you. We can plead insanity. I believe your friend Probst will plead that."

"And Sophie?"

"I'm not here to discuss your sister. Frankly, I think you must have been insane. Anyone who, shall we say, commits suicide when he has your evident talents . . ." When Hans made no comment, he reached inside his brief-case and took out a sheaf of papers, unfolding and flattening them against his lap. He said nothing more for a while, but held the papers under the light, shuffling them around, humming, pausing from time to time to stroke his chin. "I see you were in Russia last summer with a student medical detachment near the front lines. Perhaps you suffered shell shock, concussion. It says here, too, you served in France during the summer campaign in 1940. You're cited for bravery under fire. Perhaps some lingering trauma, some emotional decay. I wish you could fill me in on the details. You and the rest of the medical students at the University were conscripted into a student's company in February, 1940. Correct?"

"That's right," Hans said. A uniform and God's holy oath of loyalty to the Führer had been imposed upon them so that war could become a generous laboratory for their studies. Christl had brooded over the oath, saying it had diminished his soul. Alex had treated the swearing in as a joke, but to Hans it was a small price

74

for the chance of staying in the classroom for another term.

"Then," continued the attorney, "after the spring semester, your company was shipped out as medical orderlies to the Western Front."

Victory was already in the air, unbelievable victory over France, when Hans had gone to the railroad station. No brass bands or girls with flowers saw him off. Only his father was present, clearing his throat as Hans made a scrambling dash down the station platform. Poor Father. To remember him there, thin, prematurely aged, and feeling distractedly for something in his jacket pocket, forced a glitter into Hans's eyes. He would have been a better son never to have been born.

"Correct me if I'm in error. Your train crossed the border near Saarbrücken. From there you marched."

"With ambulances," Hans corrected. "We took turns riding. You see, the front was moving very rapidly."

"Yes, yes. Then at a small town beyond the Meuse, near Verdun . . . What I am interested in is an incident that took place there. Can you recall it?"

The helmet on his head had been an offense to springtime, and the war, if there still was one, had ceased to mutter below the horizon. There had been a battle, a grinding affair that chewed up men and turned them into carrion. Dead still lay beside the road, no more related to living things than stones. Only the occasional straggle of prisoners suggested victory over martial France. The ghost of Napoleon had not lingered in those sad peasants, who looked as though they lived on hard cheese and bitter wine.

"I'm specifically interested in what happened to you

**75**

in that village. What you did. How you reacted. It had been shelled preparatory to the advance of our armor. That was some time before you arrived, yes? You were on foot at the time. The citation indicates that you bivouacked there."

Hans remembered Christl exclaiming, "There's the reason we didn't see a church steeple. God must not have loved this town." At the end of the street lay a church. It was the only building that had been demolished, and it seemed an anachronism under the soft blue sky that streamed overhead; a softer, milkier sky than Germany's. So, too, appeared the old British Hurricane that drifted above them, seeming to dip its wing in greeting until it swept down out of the lazy sunshine with rattling guns.

Twice it passed overhead while the ground quivered like the crust of a pudding. Hans had felt like a small hunted animal, sucking his flanks in and out with fear. If he had ever doubted it before, Hans knew then that he was a coward, without the heart for killing or the stomach for a fight. When he had looked up for the first time, above the red haze of roadside flowers, he had seen Alex dive for cover. He had forgotten about Christl, who might be dead without his knowing. "Christl!" he had shouted, and felt a hand tighten reassuringly on his ankle.

"Right here, Hans."

"You all right?"

"Muddy, and scared."

"I thought I was the only one."

"When I think about Herta and the children, I'm the worst coward in the world."

Alex had crawled toward them, grinning. As the plane

again cast its lean shadow down the street, he lay on his back behind a column, fumbling with a pack of cigarettes as death whined overhead.

Impatiently, the lawyer interrupted Hans's memories. "Not so many extraneous details, Scholl. I only want to know what you did of merit. I presume the plane finally left. I presume there were casualties. You heard someone yelling for a medic."

"That's right. I heard them shouting, and we ran." In the square a crowd had formed around a wounded man. He'd been hit by bullets in the arm and throat. While Christl and Alex had applied a tourniquet to the shattered limb, Hans had found a handkerchief and clasped it over the man's throat. Unable to utter a sound, the injured man had stared beyond him through wide-open eyes at something Hans could not see.

Horrified at the dark seepage through his fingers, Hans for the first time found himself trying to comfort a dying man. "You'll make it! Hang on!" If it had been the artery, he would have been dead already. How much fluid did a human body contain? How long did it take an ambulance to drive three kilometers? "Any minute now," he had promised. "There'll be a doctor. You're not really bad. Just faint." The man had made a tight, narrow slit of his lips. "Hold on to me. You're not going to leave that pretty girl of yours." Papers lay strewn about the wounded soldier, among them a photograph of a fair, wide-eyed girl.

Here again the lawyer intruded. "While you were waiting for the ambulance, another enemy plane attacked. It says here that you didn't leave your patient."

"I don't know. I don't recall the plane." The bullets

had become no more than vagrant bees in his memory. "He would have died if I'd left him."

Hans felt the wounded man's gaze now fixed upon his face. He dared not move lest he sever an invisible lifeline. They waited in ghastly tableau until the second fighter plane exhausted its ammunition and the refueled ambulance arrived, disgorging orderlies, a stretcher, and a surgeon. "Good work," the doctor had addressed Hans. "You may have saved his life." He had begun sewing flesh like a cobbler. Hans had watched shakily, his stomach rebelling. As the laden stretcher started toward the ambulance, he had collected the papers and the picture, running after the bearers and stuffing the material into the wounded soldier's breast pocket. "You'll make it," he had said. The man had stared up at the sky out of which the plane had come. He had seemed to smile. Perhaps he saw the girl there.

Feeling sick but elated, Hans had watched the ambulance drive out of sight. He had saved a life. This revelation sustained him only briefly. Then he was assailed by a splitting headache. He was drenched with blood and terribly thirsty, and by the time he reached the village pump he was trembling all over. The pump was still working and the water ran from his sleeves red as wine.

Once the water cleared, Hans sat down. Not far off lay the ruined church. It was certainly old, and might have once been full of treasures, the sort of place he would have enjoyed browsing through with a guidebook. Then Alex arrived to break the spell. Trucks were coming up, and tanks with them. "We'll be going, Hans. You can't do any good here." They started back. "I just heard what happened to that church, Hans. It was after the French army retreated. Some fanatical Nazi colonel had rolled an immense railroad cannon up to within a few kilometers. No resistance, no sign of life but the birds in the trees, so naturally he let go with that great gun of his. Ten times. He missed on the first few, so the congregation had a chance to run for shelter down into the crypt. About then he'd found the range."

"But why? Why? He ought to be court-martialed."

"Nearly was, so I hear," continued Alex. "Then it came out that he'd made an honest mistake. The church had rather a round dome. Some restoration had been going on, scaffolding sort of like a six-pointed star. The good colonel had taken the church for a synagogue. All was forgiven."

The panzers arrived first, sixteen Mesozoic monsters moving nose to tail. There was an earthquake as they passed that cracked cobblestones, sent china crashing onto kitchen floors, and left pictures of Marshall Pétain hanging aslant. They were rolling to Cambrai and from there toward Dunkirk. Behind them had come infantry. There was a mathematical poetry to their pace that gave cadence and symmetry to the haphazardness of violent death. Hans had always enjoyed a parade, and he felt a reluctant pride as the ranks went by. This was the army that had smashed the French within two weeks and had the English backed up against the Channel. He had felt that pride, and at the same instant knew it was insane.

"Well, Scholl," the lawyer broke in, "your impressions are very vivid. I think we might stress your cool performance under fire, but frankly, it would be convenient to the Party if you pleaded insanity. Insanity would be so much more intelligible to your judges. Such a plea might

79

very well postpone your demise, which, as things stand at the moment, is a vivid possibility."

Hans sat dumbly. He was exhausted from hunger and cold and weariness, and he felt his dislike for the attorney beginning to dominate his equanimity. His impulse was never to address the man again, but to do so would be to throw away his last hope.

"You mean," Hans said finally, "if I agree, I can be certified insane. There'd be no trial?"

"Quite possibly not."

"And you could arrange this?"

"I have influence."

"But I understood that the certified insane were subject to the euthanasia program. Purification of the race, and all that."

"Well, yes. That's true," the attorney admitted. "But that is a slow process, and while there's life . . . you know. I take it you're acquainted with the euthanasia policy."

"Yes, I've heard about it." Hans had learned about the program one summer soon after leaving the Hitler Youth. It had been a grand summer of long week-end hikes, horseback rides, and preparations for medical school. He was growing more friendly with Christl and Alex, who had enrolled at the same university. Sophie, too, had been busy and happy that summer. She had always been a healer and a nurse at heart; broken dolls at first, then butterflies drowning in mud puddles, stray cats and limping chickens, fledglings cast down from crowded nests. She was quick and sure and comforting at removing splinters and bandaging cuts. If any member of her family was sick, she was eager to attend. That summer, when she had been offered an opportunity by the Sisters of Mercy at

Schwabisch Hall to work among retarded children, she had leaped at the chance. She had gone to the job gladly and written home with enthusiasm. Then suddenly she had quit, and returned to Ulm in a dark and brooding mood.

Even when Hans questioned her, she was unwilling to explain.

"I can't talk about it, Hans. I can't make myself believe what's going on there." Then one day she had broken down and told him everything. "I didn't know about it at first. They called it 'relocation' when the SS came in their black trucks and took a few children at a time. The children kept asking me where the trucks went, and I said to another home, to a better hospital, until last week I found out. They take the little ones to be gassed in the woods. O, God, Hans. How can people do such things? And I deserted them."

"I don't blame you for quitting, Sophie."

"I spoke to a doctor. He said he'd stop it. They'd take the children over his dead body. That's exactly what he said. I was with him when the SS came next time. We barred the door. I held on to the molding until my fingernails were broken, but they dragged me away, Hans. They threw me into a closet. When one of the nurses finally let me out, the doctor had gone. He had completely vanished, and a dozen children with him. What can you tell little children when they want to know where the trucks are going? I tried saying they went to heaven. I don't know what to do, Hans. Help me."

"There isn't anything you can do, Sophie, unless you want to vanish like the doctor."

"Something has to be done."

"I know, Sophie. But you mustn't work there anymore."

"I was told not to come back. But that's no answer, Hans." And he knew it wasn't. If there had been a right answer in 1938, they would not be in prison now.

Suddenly the attorney leaned forward and tapped Hans on the wrist.

"I really must get home now. There's a party I have to attend. Please answer me. Will you or will you not plead insanity?"

"It's just another form of death sentence, isn't it?" Hans asked.

"It's precisely for that attitude . . ."

"That I'm to be executed?"

". . . about to be tried," corrected the lawyer. He wagged his head sadly. "I take it you are rejecting my suggestion?"

"What sort of court?" asked Hans.

"The People's Court. Consider yourself lucky. The action of the Gestapo is not often subject to judicial review."

"One way or another, I'm dead."

Since the Reichstag fire trial, Hans had heard of the People's Court, the Volksgerichtshof. Party-dominated, its trials were in camera and without appeal. He had the prospects of a heretic before the auto-da-fé.

"You are not 'dead,' as you so crudely put it. Not if you plead insanity successfully. There is a long waiting list for euthanasia, and in your case, time is life. Think about it for a moment." It was plain the lawyer was again principally concerned about his son's broken toy. He kept working it about in its paper wrappings. "Well, Scholl, what do you say?"

"I'm not insane," Hans protested.

"Naturally you would say that. The insane always do.

Only a sane man in your position would have the sense to plead insanity."

Uncertain what to do, Hans needed time to think, to find out Sophie's intentions. "Are prisoners here allowed visitors?" he asked.

"Never on week ends. You'd have been better off trying your prank on a Monday." The lawyer rolled his thumbs and watched them tumble over and over. He looked at his watch, folded his glasses, and said, "That will be all. I shan't keep you any longer." He went to the small sink and washed his hands. "Let me know if you have any second thoughts, Scholl. Otherwise, I will see you in court."

"You may wash your feet as well."

The lawyer forced his face into a smile. "My feet do tend to sweat a bit. It's hereditary. I've tried lotions and powders, but nothing works, really," he explained with some dignity. "I should think you could manage a bit more tact when commenting on someone else's misfortunes."

"And on your son's birthday, at that. I am truly sorry." Hans felt no real malice toward his departing solicitor.

The day passed slowly. Although Hans could not see from the window, he was aware of midday and the greater brightness in which the prison lay. Somewhere, down corridors, behind locked doors, a grunt rose to a scream, then to a shriek as thin and sharp as a needle. In his imagination Hans escaped, passing through the high bars across the street and into the shady gardens. There all human sounds were lost in the hush of the meandering Isar River on its slow journey to the sea.

# CHAPTER SIX

● The temptation to change his mind was strong. With his good service record, a plea of insanity would at least gain him time, and time was everything with the war going against Germany. It couldn't last more than a year or two at most, and there were more pressing demands than the liquidation of deranged veterans. He need only survive until peace came again. Peace. Hans began to daydream of a world at peace: Brahms on the radio, not Wagner; fireworks at night, not bombs. And his patients would be old ladies with hypochondria needing sugar pills, not young erupted bodies, needing blood and a Bible. If pleading insanity was the only way, surely . . . and yet it might only be a lawyer's trick to humiliate and discredit what he had done and what he still believed was right. They might kill him anyway. There was no secret about the laboratories where human guinea pigs languished with hideous diseases and died unmourned and unremembered. There might be some other, better way. He was young, and youth is sometimes pardoned. There was his medical experience in France and Russia. God knows they needed healers more than ever. Even his motive had been patriotic: the love of Germany. Someone might understand that.

Until midafternoon his thoughts seesawed back and forth. He gazed at his face in the cell's small steel mirror and the eyes gazed back at him blank as an owl's. And then there was a third eye, an apprehension at first and then a certainty, curious, patient, regarding him from the spy hole in the door. He stared at the eye and the eye stared back at him, and finally very solemnly winked. Then the door grated open, and the lean interrogator stood alone on the threshold.

"Why, Scholl. Nice to find you home. May I come in? You seem to be keeping fit. I wish I could say the same for your friend Probst."

"What have you done to him?"

"Nothing. Nothing at all. There has been no need. I trust the occasion will not arise in your case, either. Hans, we have assembled certain evidence; books with your underlinings, your notes. The handwriting checks."

"I don't deny any of that. It is all my work."

"Of course your sister insists it was all her doing. But in the light of this evidence, Hans, it would simplify matters if you would sign a confession."

"I've denied nothing concerning myself," Hans told him.

"What I have in mind," said the interrogator, "is a confession of guilt. An admission of having done wrong. It might be very important to you should the issue of clemency or mitigation arise."

"What I did was no crime."

86

"Well, I won't press the subject just yet. I'm really here, you might say, for an off-the-record chat. Honestly, you and Sophie are a very remarkable pair of young people. If you have the time, Hans, and it looks as though you do, I'm curious about something. Strictly from a fatherly viewpoint. How did you get started with this business? Correct me if I'm wrong. It's been almost a year since the first "White Rose" leaflet came out. Did the name occur to you because of the rose on certain Tarot cards? I suppose you know those are all the death cards; the cards of dishonor, Hans. How did it feel when you first saw your own leaflets blowing about Munich? I can hardly imagine."

Hans heard and did not hear. Starved for sleep, he moved once again in that springtime street behind the University. There was the usual clamorous exodus from class, the loud discussion, and then the hush of finding the first leaflets. He had looked for reaction in the faces of strangers. Surprise, anger, delight were all there, often mixed, until a squad of SS pushed through, confiscating leaflets and routing the crowd of students. In the quiet backwater of a nearby parking lot built on the site of St. Matthew's Church, he found Sophie reading her first leaflet. Just turned twenty, she had been in Munich only a few weeks, and she was studying under Professor Huber of the Philosophy Department. She read with utter concentration. Hans could hardly rouse her.

"Have you seen this, Hans? It's wonderful!" She thrust the leaflet into his hands. "Whoever did this deserves the Knight's Cross. Hallelujah!"

"Perhaps it's a step in the right direction," he said thoughtfully. "A rather short one."

87

"More than that! More than that!" she insisted. "I wish I knew who did this. I'd give anything to work with them."

"Your life, Sophie?"

"Anything, if I could do some good."

"Sophie, a little thing like this won't change the world."

"I know, but it's a way of keeping the world from changing you."

"Unless you're caught. I've heard the guillotine makes quite a distinct alteration. Listen to me, Sophie. If you should ever find out who these foolish people are, promise me you won't get involved."

She answered instead, "Hans, you could at least be happy about it."

"I am happy," he told her. "That there's only one like me and only one like you."

"And one like Alex."

"Three musketeers."

"Unique."

"Without peers."

"Marvelous types . . . oh, oh," she said. "Here comes an old friend."

"Hans! Sophie! What luck seeing you. I didn't know you were both in Munich."

It was Franz Bittner, ghost-white and childlike still, in a Death's Head cap and a stiff black uniform that seemed to support his small body like armor.

"It's been so long. Sophie, you're more lovely than ever." Indeed, though her clothing was serviceable and far from glamorous, Sophie did look lovely. It occurred to Hans with surprise that she also looked maternal. Her face was reassuring in repose, beautiful in animation.

"I used to worship you from afar," Franz admitted.

88

"That's nice, Franz," she said, but she did not sound as though it were very nice at all.

Hans extended his hand and Franz took it, not shaking it, but holding it lightly as if to feel its weight.

"Hans, this is good. You look fine."

"You, too, Franz." Hans felt himself incapable of cordiality, not so much toward his old friend as toward the uniform he wore.

"Hans, I see you have one of those White Rose things. Please let me take it. You could be picked up just for reading something like that. Nasty interrogation by the Gestapo, I don't know what ugly consequences." Franz took the leaflet and studied it. Thoughtfully he read aloud:

" 'Nothing is less worthy of a civilized country than passively to allow itself to be *governed* by an irresponsible gang of bosses who have surrendered to their lower instincts.' Oh, this is poetic!" His eyes skipped down the sheet. "And this: 'If each one of us waits for the other to begin, the messengers of avenging nemesis . . .' That's really classic! '. . . will draw closer and closer, until the last victim has been thrown in vain into the jaws of the insatiable monster.' Hans, seriously, what do you make of this? What do they want? Revolution? Chaos? Just listen to the ending. 'At the temple portals, we shout aloud in ecstasy: Freedom! Freedom!' Good God, Hans, it's an embarrassing thing to read. And to think that probably some poor deluded bohemian with a beard and oil paints on his cuffs is risking his life to write it."

He balled the leaflet up and let it fall. "For your own good, both of you," he said gently. "I speak through fondness only."

89

Sophie was the first to withdraw. Saying that she had a lecture, she knelt down, retrieved the crumpled leaflet, said an emphatic good-bye, and departed.

"I can't help but like her," Franz said. "The way she courts trouble . . . Well, Hans, let me walk you home. How is your father? Another individualist, your father."

Hans replied that his father was fine. He dared say no more, for Franz Bittner, who had never had any occasion to straighten his back in self-esteem, stood squarely before him now, legs spread, boots planted. Quite obviously he had found himself in the Death's Head SS. Hans dared not speak to such a man about a father who had not discovered hate until he had discovered Hitler; whose days were spent in smoldering denunciation of the anti-Christ, whose nights focused on clandestine listening to the BBC.

They had begun to walk in the direction of Schwabing.

"Honestly Hans, this is luck." Franz's mirthless chuckles were like stones rattling in an empty pail.

"And you, Franz. You're at Dachau, aren't you? Do you like it?"

Franz gave a secret smile of amusement. "Do you mean, how does it feel being the wolf at the slaughterhouse gate? It's an odd feeling. We home-front warriors are resented, you know. But I tell myself, what's the sting of resentment compared to that of a Russian bullet?"

Except for chilling rumors, Hans knew little about Dachau or the other concentration camps. According to his father, in every stable at Auschwitz-Berkenau, a thousand humans had replaced fifty horses. True, the newspapers gave the lie to such tales. With his own eyes he had seen the photographs of smiling young Jews striding off to sanctuaries in Warsaw and Amsterdam, but could one trust the pictures? Propaganda, like the Great Wall of

90

China, blotted out every horizon. But even in Munich the yellow park benches were almost empty, and he had read the removal notices. "Secret State Police, Munich Headquarters, to so and so. You are to hold yourself in readiness." Here a date and hour would be filled in. When that date and hour had passed, another flat or house would be empty, and only the white eagle and the swastika on the door would remain to tell of what had happened. *"Arbeit macht frei,"* (Work makes you free) was inscribed on the wrought-iron gates of Dachau, but those who walked through them never returned. Nor was Franz about to divulge any secrets. To Hans's questions he answered cryptically, "You know our motto, 'Being is more than seeming.' " He repeated the phrase thoughtfully as though testing it in his mind, as one would test a rapier for keenness. "I can tell you this, Hans. Short of Russia, I'd take any sort of transfer. Actually, I've been trying to get shifted here to Munich. You know, that little prison out at Stadelheim."

There Roehm had died, and Hans himself had been confined for six weeks of uncertainty. "I've heard of the place," he said.

"Speaking of Russia," said Franz, "I hear old Otto has gotten himself shipped out there with one of Himmler's action groups. Stupid idiot. Did it ever occur to you that Otto spelled backward is Otto? Doesn't that exactly describe his mentality?"

Franz had developed a habit of leaning forward while he talked as if reaching out for understanding and sympathy. "Not that I intend to cast aspersions on the Russian campaign. We shall certainly win there, as we have everywhere else."

"The latest slogan says, 'Over the graves, forward.'

What happens when the whole world's a cemetery?"

"Come now, Hans. That's defeatism. You can say such things to me, but . . ."

"I've spent a long time in hospitals, Franz. One gets the impression the official casualty rates are rather modest."

"Naturally, there's a price, Hans. But look at it this way. The individual is imperfect, yes? He must die sooner or later. But we Germans, taken together, will not die. If one lacked confidence in the ultimate triumph of the German race, every sacrifice, everything that we stand for would seem outright lunacy. That's why I object to these pamphlets. Basically they're harmless, but they do no good, they only delude. They condemn, but they offer no solutions. Ah, well, you have studies, I have a train to catch. We must do our duty." Franz was grinning. It was impossible for Hans to decide just what he was thinking. All he knew was that little Franz had become a menace. "Well, it has been wonderful, seeing you after so long, Hans. Once I get my Munich assignment, we must have a real talk. Dinner perhaps. Say we will."

"I have a favorite place," Hans said. "Italian. You'll like it."

Hans felt giddy once he had climbed to the apartment. For a moment he collapsed in a chair, thinking, "We've done it now. We're committed, I don't know to what." Maybe it was all foolishness, as Franz had implied. He didn't want to think about it just then. Getting up, he washed his face and studied himself in the mirror, seeing a strong, angry face there. Do I always look angry, he wondered. I ought to spend more time studying. I ought to spend some time with girls. He had never really been in love. Just then he wanted to be in love with a girl who was in love with him, preferably a beautiful laughing Italian girl with long dark hair. He touched his own face, flesh, bones, the eager pulse of life in his forehead. It was a good face, really; strong and well cut when it relaxed. If he could only walk by the Isar with a girl on his arm and no problems. What mattered, really, was being alive. Alive in springtime. He went to the window to breathe in the damp earth, the first flowers. The bitter, acrid smell of the fires from the bombing still hung in the air. But it was the beginning of another year, and he felt very much alive.

With the Gestapo never far from his mind, the heavy knocking at the apartment door reverberated inside his chest. His first instinct was to plunge through the window, but that was four flights to concrete.

The voice reassured him. "Hans, open up. It's me. Let me in."

Sophie, books under one arm, papers under the other, looked angry and puzzled.

"Sorry," he said. "I must have locked up."

"This," she said, prodding at a paper document with one finger as though testing a dangerous creature with a stick for signs of life. "Hans, you did this. And you never told me." She slapped him hard across the face with the rolled-up pamphlet. The sound of it rang across the hall. Not really hurt but too astonished to move, Hans heard the sharp intake of Sophie's breath, saw her wide-open eyes above the hand that she had clapped over her own mouth, as if what she had done shocked her as much as it had surprised him.

Hans shook his head to clear it. He stuttered, "Sophie, what . . . what in heaven's name was that for?"

She had half turned from him, her hands clenched together at her waist, an obstinate desperation in her forehead and chin which seemed to say, "How dare you look so innocent!"

She's a stranger, he thought, with reactions I cannot fathom. I don't know her. I don't know my own sister.

"Why did you do it, Hans? If your own life means nothing, what about your friends? You told me to keep away from such people, and then you go right ahead, secretly turning yourself into some kind of outlaw. Hans, why? If you won't think of yourself, think of Mother." Again she brandished the White Rose leaflet in his face, then she balled it up and threw it down, one copy among hundreds which he had written, a protest against Hitler so emphatic that his authorship, if discovered, could cost him his life.

Feigning ignorance no longer, he said, "So Alex told you. I wish he hadn't."

"He didn't. I wish he had. He doesn't trust me either. I'm not a child, Hans. Why wouldn't you trust me?"

Hans looked down the corridor to the stairs, which were empty. He picked up the leaflet. It must not be found there. "Come inside, Sophie, and don't shout. People will hear." He closed the door behind them and locked it. She knew, and should not know. How had he been so careless? If she could find out, why not the Gestapo?

## CHAPTER SEVEN

The slim interrogator stood up, paced to the sink and back, sat down. "Then I take it," he said, "your sister was against this pamphleteering, and you seduced her into it."

"That's exactly right," Hans agreed, hoping it might help her in court. "She's younger than me, and impressionable." But it wasn't true. She had followed his lead in many things, but once her mind was made up, Sophie seldom changed it. She went further than he did. Rarely could she see two sides to any issue, and even when she saw them she became instantly and dogmatically partisan.

What happened to defenseless people she felt also happened to her, and Hans sensed that since the euthanasia episode her last inner struggles had been resolved. When she arrived in Munich to study "Leibnitz and the Justification of God" under Professor Huber, he had met her at the railroad station. "Good God, Sophie," he had exclaimed, hefting her suitcase.

"No, just books," she had replied. "But there's something about God inside there I want you to see." Although not raised as a Catholic she had done much Catholic reading. Hans knew she admired the pamphlets of Bishop Galen of Munster, which had been circulated protesting the Party's extermination of the mentally retarded.

"You're taking a chance carrying those pamphlets, aren't you?" he said. "It's against the law."

"Not against God's law."

"I'm not an expert on God's law, Sophie. But whether or not it's evil to put mental defectives out of their misery is a matter of opinion."

"Hans, you don't believe that."

And of course he did not, for they were kindred spirits up to a point. They saw the same devil even if they did not see the same God.

"This way," he directed her. "We'll take a tram."

When the streetcar finally arrived with its lugubrious blackout glass, a crowd rushed for it, willing to trample or be trampled for a seat. Hans and Sophie did not make it, and they walked. Hans carried the heavy suitcase, first in one hand, then in the other. By the time they arrived at his flat, they were sharing the load between them.

Alex had been waiting for them there. "At last! The beautiful Sophie Scholl!" was his greeting.

"Shut up, you liar," she answered, but Hans could tell they were glad to see one another again.

"One little kiss," pleaded Alex.

"You idiot!"

"Just one, on the eyelid."

She looked at him, trying to appear angry.

"All right; the ear lobe."

"Alex, I think your anatomy lessons have gone to your head."

"Sophie, this is our home. At least have a look around," Hans urged.

"It's wonderful, Hans," she said without a glance about the small apartment. "But first, I've got something I want you both to hear." And she read aloud from the bishop's speech that condemned Party repression of the Church and the increasing practice of euthanasia for the insane and retarded. "Well?" she concluded. "What do you think? No wonder they call him the Lion of Munster."

Alex had listened carefully, massaging the side of his face with the flat of his hand. "And yet he wears paper collars."

"Shabby or not, the man has courage. He's not afraid of giants."

"Don't you mean windmills?" replied Alex.

"You don't always have to joke," Sophie objected. "I say, thank God someone has the courage to speak out. If I were a man . . ." How often Hans heard her use that phrase. "If I were a man, I'd get some sort of duplicating set and spread copies of his speech all over Germany."

"When you talk like that, so earnestly, you sound remarkably young. If you want to appear older, Sophie, let your hair grow longer and coil it at the nape of your neck," Alex said "It would be a becoming way to wear it."

"Shut up, Alex. If I were a man, I'd give you a black eye. I would."

"My dear, pretty girl, thank God you're not."

"I would have his sermon printed and I would drop it all over Germany from a plane. And I'm not your dear pretty girl."

"No, you're my golden princess, and I'm mad about you."

"And where would you get a plane?" asked Hans. "I understand Herr Goering requires a permit for flying kites."

"Then I'd use a balloon."

"Ha. They say Goering is deadly with a bow and arrow," said Alex. "Truthfully, Hans, you shouldn't give your sister such scary ideas."

"She gets them from Father," was Hans's resigned comment.

"These days I don't know how you two find everything so laughable."

"Sophie, you must try harder," said Alex, "but if you will be somber, must one be an archbishop, or a pope with divisions behind him, to put out a newsletter? Not at all. You don't need a plane. A rudimentary sense of the language and a pen, perhaps a taste for suicide. Be a little bit mad. Like us, eh, Hans?" Hans said that prison had done a lot to cure him of insanity, but Alex was not to be silenced. "Sophie, I wonder about you. Suppose the German people were starving and you could become wheat so that they could eat and be saved. Would you do it?"

"Who wouldn't?" said Sophie. "Of course. We all would."

"Softer," cautioned Hans. "Our Blockleiter's always on the prowl, and the keyholes in this building are extra large. His ear just fits."

98

It had all been talk at first. When it came to action, Hans had drafted, printed, and distributed leaflets without Sophie's knowledge, but it was not he so much that had acted as the idealized self she had made of him. And then, when he had expected her applause, if no one else's, she had rewarded him with a slap in the face.

They had come to no understanding that night. Sophie had retired to her own room, and if she cried, there was no sound. The following day began with a biology class at 8:15, skimmed milk and powdered egg about nine, then the dissecting room to help breakfast settle. Great arching ceilings, bare bulbs, and the blue-white corpse of some derelict laid out with no trace of dignity. Alex joked as usual, but no one enjoyed that part of medical school. Hans had returned to the apartment for lunch because they could not afford to waste food. Sophie was there, too, and necessities were spoken in flat, emotionless tones. Hans had tried to study on his bed, but instead gazed at the sunspots on the floor while she persecuted the luncheon dishes. "Sophie," he had muttered to himself. Then, "Women!" She had withdrawn into the mystique of the female mind. She had always been so direct and uncomplicated, so sympathetic to his endeavors. Now, when he had done something which she had for so long applauded in the abstract, she slapped him down. Was there some defect in her own courage? Hans felt an odd satisfaction that she could disappoint him. He was certain he had often disappointed her, and would again.

He attended chemistry laboratory in the late afternoon, but not before he realized that her discovery had come through his own carelessness. A volume of Schiller, with the passages he had marked for inclusion in the leaflet, lay open on his desk. He would not make that mistake again. Again! His pamphleteering was over, finished!

That night, there was still no communication. She was suffering from a persecution mania, he decided. Eating supper too quickly, he developed indigestion and went for a solitary stroll, calling out as he left, "What are we going to do? Hate each other for the rest of our lives?" Then he banged the door firmly behind his back and kicked a pebble for two blocks until he lost it. By the time he decided to return home, he was himself lost.

The following morning, Sophie had departed before he arose. What suggested a change in mood was his razor, meticulously cleaned, and paste squeezed and waiting on his toothbrush. He did not see her throughout the day, and by evening the radio was reporting raiders flying south. The low lamentations of the city sirens, announcing one of Munich's air alerts, propelled Hans home. The apartment was dark and deserted. The sirens of the first alarm fell silent. He went to the window and looked down into the street, where a few figures hastened to shelter. It was only a first alert. All the city lights were out, as they were every night now. Somewhere a dog barked. Far off the mountains edged the horizon like frosted glass, and the moon climbed over them, pale and fully round.

Anger rose in Hans, anger that sprang from concern for his sister. They would not as yet have left for the shelter, but he told himself they should have gone long ago. Sophie's disregard was endangering them both. When she finally came, he was caught off guard. "Oh, Hans, I was afraid you wouldn't be here." Instead of a rehearsed reprimand, he suggested they go to the shelter. "It's so stuffy and crowded," she replied.

"But safe."

"I'd go if I were alone."

"We can't protect each other from bombs," he reminded her.

"We need to talk, Hans, and we can't down there. You will talk?"

"Of course. Would you like to hear about the close shave I had this morning?"

"What happened, Hans? Gestapo?"

"Hardly. A close shave with a razor."

"A razor?" Then she understood and laughed, a loud boyish laugh that made slits of her eyes.

"Hush," Hans cautioned her. "The air-raid warden will hear you." But the ice was broken. They would have their talk.

"I've behaved abominably," she admitted.

"I'm the one," he replied, though privately he agreed with her.

"No, there's no excuse for me, really. But I want to explain why I've been such a bitch. When I found one of your books all underlined and marked up with notes, the same words as those in the leaflet . . . well, I knew. I knew you'd written it, and maybe Alex, too. I tried to tell myself it wasn't fair, putting us in danger. But it wasn't being trusted by either of you that made me mad. I felt such a child. You let me babble like a silly idiot while you were actually doing something. What a baby I must have seemed to you. No wonder you didn't want me to know."

The long lamentation of the second alert rose over the city, a slithering snake of sound.

"They're coming this way," Hans said. "You still want to stay here?"

Sophie joined him at the window. Figures scurried in the

moonlight, their shadows sliding before them. Above, stars swam in the sky like silver minnows. "Just look at those stars," he said, "and the clouds." Clouds had grouped themselves around the rising moon as if preparing themselves for an assumption.

But Sophie was on a scent and not to be diverted. "You didn't do it all alone, Hans, did you?"

Reluctantly he turned from the window. "No. There's Alex, and Christl, too. We'd talked about doing something for ages. Then you came along with the bishop's sermons. Well, we all chipped in and bought a small hectograph. Just type up a draft, bang, bang, slide in the sheet, pull over the lever, pull out the paper. We were like three kids playing at newspapermen. Kid stuff, until you imagine the Gestapo bursting in. Alex and I took the leaflets around at night. I'm damned glad it's over."

"I remember how late you were that night, and how you were laughing."

"With relief."

"I should have guessed," Sophie said.

"So I've made a little gesture, Sophie, and maybe I feel better. But that's the end of it. Honestly, working with Alex is terrifying. He's a clown. Up to all sorts of giddy tricks. He'd walk a tightrope over a bottomless pit. I can't play at this sort of thing. It's too dangerous."

"Hans, from now on I'll help you. I'll do anything you wish."

"Listen, don't complicate my life, please. I haven't been able to sleep decently. I can hardly study. And besides, it's no activity for women."

"We're half the human race, Hans. I want to help."

"Don't push, Sophie. Don't push." They stood face to

face in the moonlight. Outside, long strands of light reached toward the stars. "Suppose our handbill was a big hit. The students loved it, but what did it accomplish? Nothing. Nothing at all, and it scared me nearly to death."

"It did your conscience good."

"Maybe, but it played hell with my stomach." Searchlights stitched across the night sky. The beams of light converged, crossed and divided. "The trouble with you, Sophie, is that you believe in miracles. I remember when you were small you always wanted to perform a miracle. Heal a blind doll, or something. Remember? But miracles don't happen."

"I think you and Alex and Christl are a bit of a miracle."

"Sophie, we've never discussed another leaflet. We planned only the one."

"It may be useless and foolhardy, as you say, Hans, but it's so right at the same time. It's just a beginning."

Above the city searchlights had begun to sweep back and forth more frantically, clear and sharp, tunneling the blackness. Here and there they entered a cloud and were lost, like a lantern dropping into a dark lake. The silence of the city was oppressive. Then, far off, as hushed as the drag of pebbles in a quiet surf, came the noise of bombers, drowned abruptly by the high incisive note of fighter planes, interceptors moving with unnatural speed over Munich.

To the north, the battle had begun as the heavenly host was greeted by the first endless chains of antiaircraft tracers. Mere humans seemed to be casting up net to capture divine messengers of doom.

A blue flare opened overhead, turning the scene into

**103**

a charcoal engraving. Hans and Sophie heard with indifferent ears the first concussion of the bombs and the constant drone of motors in the sky, for the immediate danger of the raid was eclipsed by the hazard of their own thoughts. A solitary figure jogged down the street. Policeman? Warden? Perhaps an outcast like them.

Thus far the raids on Munich had been token. According to Party declaration, they would soon vanish. So officially the medical students were to continue their studies uninterrupted. Unofficial plans were to use their skills in the hospitals and rescue squads after the raids. If the bombings continued, this might be the last raid Hans could watch impersonally, measuring the enemy he would soon resist.

Flak batteries chattered from the rooftops of the city, but by now the ears and nerves had begun to tune themselves to the whistle and the roar. "I'm not afraid, Hans!" Sophie shouted into her brother's ear. "I'm not!" She put her hands out of the window to catch the moonlight like honey in her steady fingers.

"I am afraid," he said, but she did not hear him in the tumult.

Amid the converging beams of light a plane hung like a silver toy upon a Christmas tree. Beaded tracers wafted leisurely toward it. One moment it was there, and the next instant the glowing ash of a cigarette seemed to have been flung down from the sky. The searchlights moved off on other errands, but somewhere, in some dark field, a propeller would be planted like a snapped sword.

Now the raid was ending. One by one the strands of artificial light were vanishing, to be replaced by stars.

"How wonderful," said Sophie. "They're the eyes of God."

"That's the all-clear," Hans said. The raid and their talk had left him feeling bludgeoned.

"You know my professor, Huber? He's marvelous, Hans. We all bang our pencils on our desks when he comes in to talk, and the Student League people sit there white with rage. They can't do a thing! I've told you how he speaks to us after class. I'm sure he'll help. He's—."

"Absolutely not, Sophie! You don't seem to appreciate the danger any more than Alex. We aren't going to involve another soul."

But Hans had used the word "we," and Sophie was quick to pick it up.

"We'll do it without him, then." She was suddenly radiant, as if she had received a joyous honor. Reluctantly Hans felt himself a mirror of her pleasure, for despite his arguments he had already begun to rejoice at the thought of her steadfast partnership.

"Only let me mention a few things you must think about, should we ever go on with this. I want you to understand the hazard. It will be treason, Sophie. I'm a traitor now, and you will be, too, if you should ever help me. I don't know if it's worth it. What if men are basically evil? I often believe it. Perhaps what Hitler wants for Germans is what we genuinely want for ourselves. Even if it isn't, what can our few leaflets do?"

"You saw the students, Hans. How excited they were! Many of them would help us if they could. One day, who knows, they may rise against the Nazis. So let me feel glad, Hans. You be glad too, please." Her voice was coaxing, confident, and very hard for him to resist. Between them they imagined a Germany aroused, a dictator cast down, the millennium to follow.

The last whooping siren fell silent. Between the occasional shrill clangor of fire engines and ambulances, sawing insects celebrated the night. People were returning from the shelters full of relief and weariness. It was an oddly gentle time, after a raid, and brother and sister were gentle with one another. Co-conspirators against the world, they made plans. They were traitors now, and would be hunted.

CHAPTER EIGHT

● "Damn it, Scholl! I'd like to understand you. I really would. Have you never had a sense of patriotism, of obligation? Germany gave you a good home, a fine education, yet you show no trace of gratitude. You young people simply want to obstruct, tear down. You're like these antivivisectionists. When their leaflets tell how some poor mutt with his kidneys removed licks his tormentor's hand, it's heartbreaking, but it's also without vision. If we listened to these humanitarians, we'd have no remedies for hydrophobia, typhoid . . . Scholl, did this never once occur to you? Did you never have a change of heart, second thoughts?" The interrogator looked as though he had neither slept nor eaten. His clothes hung on him like sails on a windless day.

"Yes, I had second thoughts," Hans admitted.

After the publication of the third leaflet in June of 1942, he had resolved to make an end to the White Rose.

In fact, now that Sophie was involved, the constant aura of danger had become unbearable to him. The departure of his student medical company for Russia and the summer offensive curtailed activities indefinitely, and he was relieved that for the present he could do no more.

It was an incident at the front that finally made up his mind. He remembered the quiet of that crisp September morning. He had heard the slog of boots before he saw the punishment detail to which he had been assigned as medical officer. The gloomy little column drew near. He exchanged salutes with the lieutenant in command. They rode side by side, very stiff in their saddles, part of a ritual.

"Why?" Hans had asked.

"Pardon?"

"Why is he being shot?"

"Disobedience. He was part of an execution detail, and he wouldn't shoot. Said he'd had enough killing. That's it. Might be rather fun if it weren't so damnably cold."

There was no formal place of execution. No scaffold, no solid brick wall presented itself, but they halted where a tall stump stood in the midst of nothingness. Hans was close enough to see the prisoner's face, close enough to offer him a cigarette. The condemned man took it. He was shaking slowly and steadily. He could hardly light the cigarette. Hans could make nothing of the prisoner's expression. Rigid control had frozen it into a mummer's mask. They were about the same age, similar in appearance, and they had a bond in common of which only Hans was aware. Both had sinned against the state.

"Have you something to drink" asked the prisoner.

It was startling, as though a corpse had spoken. "What's that? I'm sorry," replied Hans.

"A dose of schnapps, preferably an overdose," said the prisoner with grim humor.

Hans had none. Even if he had, there was no time for the liquor to work, nor time for the questions he wanted to ask. Would you do it all over again if you had the choice? Was it worth it? The man was already bound to the stump. He stood with eyes wide open, facing the first onrush of sunlight. Then the death cap was fitted. Hans clutched his horse by the bridle and turned his back. Could the prisoner still see the blue haze of the hills from behind the black cloth? Could he see the pearly glint of rifle barrels? Hans was walking his horse away when the report came. The horse Hans called Napoleon leaped sideways, turned a wild eye back toward Hans as though to ask, Are they shooting at us? Hans gave him a reassuring pat. It was over.

His task remained, a technicality that required him to listen, his ears plugged with the black rubber buttons of the stethoscope, his hand moving the amplifier over the riddled chest, for any fluttering sound of life. Eight bullets had been fired, and eight had struck home. "Is there something I should sign?" he asked the lieutenant, and the lieutenant gave him a sheet of paper.

Then Hans mounted Napoleon and rode back toward the field station. The late summer sun was fully up, but horse and rider shivered all the way. Before he had dismounted, Hans knew he would not be riding again for a while. Columns were moving up with a labored rhythm. Some of the panzers bore "To Moscow" signs upon their turrets. They had carried the same signs the year before.

During the next twenty-four hours the armored columns moved forward two or three kilometers. The Russians counterattacked, and the old line was re-established with heavy cost. The field surgery was kept busy for a week. Hans saw, treated, and despaired of many mutilated and dying men. Yet even this bloodbath could not wipe away the memory of the prisoner's eyes as he had faced the firing squad. What had he been thinking at the end? That it was all a dream, a mistake? That in a minute they would free him? Surely they couldn't intend to shoot him down. But they did, and he must still be lying there, blue and bloated, with only flies for company. Even flies would desert him finally. The autumn rains would cover him with brown ditch water and rotting leaves, and all that would remain would be the dim disgrace of a traitor's death.

Violent death: the one thing that silenced all. It seemed an answer to any argument. Before it, courage, honor, conscience became so many glass marbles that fathers gave to children to play with until they were lost. A man should have conscience and courage enough to say no; no to an officer's command when that command was clearly evil; no to a government's decree when that decree was corrupt. But if death was the price, such a word became expensive. And weren't there more fundamental values. A slow, deep draft of sweet night air? The steady pulse inside him? These physical sensations were precious to Hans, and he lacked the courage to put them in jeopardy again.

In Russia the first snow had come early in October, and with it came rats. Even when asleep, Hans seemed to hear the scurrying of immense rodents in the rotten structure around him; rats gnawing up from the roots of the earth. They would nibble off your toes if given the chance, and many were rabid. The medical students learned to sleep entirely wrapped in their heavy blankets, and more than ever they talked longingly of home. But when word came that they were to be shipped back to Germany before Christmas, Hans felt depressed. In Russia he had served humanity in a small way, and the perils of war were straightforward. He had found a certain peace.

The last morning Hans was shaken awake. His first consciousness was a vague troubled feeling that something was wrong. He swung his feet to the ground, wriggling his toes in an effort to warm them. As thoughts formed, he remembered he was leaving. This should have been a day of rejoicing. He stood up in the unshaded light. The washstand was full of ice. He hadn't bathed in days. Miserably he ate his powdered eggs and gristle and experienced a yearning for pleasure so great that it made him shiver.

Some of his patients would be on the train. Hans took leave of those who were remaining. Then he said goodbye to Major Kramer, who put his hand on Hans's shoulder. "You'll make a sound doctor some day, Scholl." There wasn't much else to say. Hans was going home. The major was awaiting his second sub-zero winter and a Russian offensive.

Hans ducked outside. It was a gray world, lit neither by the late moon nor the early sun. A strong wind sang over the snow. It blew steadily and evenly from the cold heart of the North Pole, and the snow it brought was not Bavarian snow, but something insidious and inexhaustible.

As they marched to the railroad siding, some sang

**111**

Christmas carols. Out of the gloom the boxcars loomed solid and black. Lamps glowed redly in the murky air. It was already below zero, and soldiers worked stiffly putting the wounded aboard. They were aided by Russian workers, recruited for industrial service, who would be taking the train to Germany. By the time the casualties were loaded, Hans no longer felt the cold. He was part of it.

When the last stretcher was aboard and the last ambulatory patient had found a seat, Hans walked through the cars. Here were the real veterans—sleepless, easily tearful men, envying Hans his wholeness and, at the same time, contemptuous of his unbloodied kind.

Except for the bandages and the weary faces, it might have been a holiday train. Geese hung from the windows, frozen solid. There were bottles of plum brandy, vodka and tinned caviar for relatives back home. Someone with two good hands played a concertina, and from the volunteer Russian workers cars there rose singing, too. But there were other cars, freight cars at the head of the train, under SS supervision. Even in the cold Hans had smelled them, and he had heard cries from behind doors that were locked and bolted on the outside. "More volunteers," he was told. But you didn't lock up volunteers that way; not even livestock bound for the slaughterhouse. Hans tried not to think about them, but he couldn't help it. Nor could he help thinking about his father, who had been arrested in August for slandering Hitler; a short sentence, Sophie had assured him by letter. But how could one be sure, when the Gestapo was involved?

The train gave a shattering jerk as though wrenching itself free from solid foundations. A thin cheer rose. They were going home. Hans moved to a frost-spangled window.

Yes, he thought, the weather reports at least were right. Snow had come to stay all over Russia. Flakes brushed against the glass and he watched them wearily, silver and gray, sweeping against the light. Hans meant to hibernate. Let the train jog on all winter; he still could not make up for sleep lost. If a patient needed help, then he would bestir himself, but not otherwise.

He had scarcely drowsed off, however, when the train stopped suddenly, throwing him to the floor. "Guerrillas! Ambush!" Rumors sped through the car, but there was nothing to see but the wind-lashed emptiness and a siding barely showing through the drifts. For some time they waited. Cars forward were uncoupled and rolled back onto the siding. Then Hans felt the train being slowly pulled forward, passing the uncoupled cars. Their doors, which had been locked before, were open now, and crowds erupted from them, driven in grotesque flight into hip-deep snow, where they labored as the SS mowed them down. Six machine guns fired into the sub-zero wastes.

Hans saw it through the train window, as ghastly and unreal as a Bosch painting come to life. He could do nothing. No doctors were allowed off the train. No pulse was taken, for what the bullets failed to do, nature would accomplish in its good time. When all was stillness outside except for the whining wind, the machine guns were dismantled for easier transport, the SS boarded the train, a whistle sounded, and the train moved off again. Already the stone-dark lumps that scattered the emptiness were dusted over with a fine chalk. Before nightfall there would be no trace. No trace, no monument, no memory. Hans felt hunger coming on—it seemed incredible, after what he had witnessed—and after eating, a deep drows-

**113**

iness. As they chugged sleepily south, Hans formed letters in the moisture on the window. "GOD" he wrote there, then rubbed it out with the side of his fist. What would God be doing out there? Perhaps Christl might tell him; Christl, who had spoken of the Catholics with derisive envy, now wrote in his letters of studying the catechism. Hans's grandfather had known the number of hairs in the Almighty's beard. He thought Sophie still had a pretty close idea. Once he had thought he knew, but the God he had expected to believe in forever was a child's God. Before coming to Russia he had written in his diary, "Had Christ not lived, and had He not died, would there be any meaning in all of this?" But how could the crucifixion, for all its pain, compare with the realities of the Russian front? No, his God was not out there with the armies. If God permitted this war, He was cruel. If He could not prevent it, He was impotent, and if He was unconscious of it all, He had reached such a level of serene beatitude as to have nothing to do with man at all.

Sophie might see God in the perfection of the falling snowflakes, but to Hans they were cruel and impartial, falling on the just and the unjust alike. God would not raise traitors from the dead. He would not raise Jews or Communists; the snow would cover them. It must lie thickly now, drifting on the wooden crosses and the trampled mounds and the unburied dead. Hans was afraid, for himself and for his family. Even now his father might lie, dishonored, among the honorable dead. Were not morality, ethics, a Christian conscience all utterly irrelevant to the reality of those stiffened limbs, those empty-socketed skulls grinning liplessly beneath the snow? Self-preservation should be a sensible man's first and only thought, but that would mean closing his mind to the concentration camps, to the locked freight cars, and to the countless future dead.

Restless and wind-whipped, the snow fell on a blank world, a world before creation. In the north, at Leningrad, which the German armies had besieged for over a year, it fell with a dry, stinging hiss. Like old, shrouded nuns, ravens fell dead of it and were eaten in Leningrad. Snow fell in every part of the gray central plain, on the tree-less hills, on stalled panzers, and on freezing men. To the south it fell more softly along the endless miles of the Don River line, all the way to Stalingrad, where it was an early, melting snow. Over three thousand jagged miles of German army the snow fell, over three million men who knew that the victory to which they were com-mitted would change the course of history. It fell upon the living and the dead, upon the backs and faces of suspected Jews and Communists beside a railroad siding forty miles from any town, upon troop trains moving north and south. Hans could hear it. Even in his sleep he could hear the falling of each feathery flake.

"I take it, then," said the slim interrogator, "that by the time you returned from Russia last autumn you had decided against further pamphleteering. A sensible de-cision; but clearly someone changed your mind. Your sister? She seems very persuasive. She has tried to win me over; a very appealing girl. Or was it your friend Schmorell? Not poor Probst, surely. None of them? Then your father. He has a bad record. I see here he was jailed for making radical statements. Is he the one?"

"I'm not incapable of making my own decisions."

115

"I see also that your father was released from prison just before you got home from Russia."

"Listen, my father had nothing to do with this. He would have talked me out of it if he could have."

"I see. Then obviously he knew about the White Rose."

"No. I simply mean he advised me to keep out of trouble. It was all very general."

"Then perhaps it would be fair to call the White Rose the work of children wanting to punish their parents; so typical of young radicals."

Again Hans objected; but in an odd way it had been his father who had unwittingly brought him back to pamphleteering.

Hans remembered arriving home from Russia. A greasy fog interspersed with squirts of rain had accompanied the train all the way from Berlin. First he saw the cathedral half lost in mist, and then the station. It was always winter in the Ulm railway station. A few soldiers were there, and an old woman pushed a coffee wagon among them. Hans had expected no reception, but Sophie, who had received his letter mailed in Berlin, was waiting. She raced toward him, running hard like a boy, her hair bobbing from side to side like a bell. When she stopped before him, they were both inarticulate. He stroked her cheek, his heart filled with the beauty of her smile. "Summer has been good to you, Sophie. You've been out in the sun."

She stared at him as if she saw a ghost. "Oh, Hans." She took his hands in hers and kissed them with clumsy force. "You look so much older."

"In Russia, you either die fast or age fast," he told her.

"It must be terrible."

"It is." Already the experience was merging into a gray dream, and it was hard to remember just how it had been.

"Hans, I missed you and Alex so. I read all your letters over and over. Alex sent caviar. He says we'll have a reunion party in Munich. I've really missed Alex, Hans. He's such a clown."

"You do like him, Sophie."

"Of course I do. Thank God he's back safe . . . and Father, too."

"Is he all right?"

"Perfectly. A little quieter, perhaps, but well."

They walked home from the station. Streetcars were impossible, slow and crowded with people, and the road was full of walking and bicycle-riding factory workers from the villages along the Danube. Sophie related the news as best she could, but since their father had destroyed the radio for fear the Gestapo would accuse him of listening to the BBC, it was more rumor than fact. Something had happened in North Africa, at El Alamain. The papers were silent about it, too silent, but Sophie had heard that all the church bells in England had rung for the first time in three years. There was even an unconfirmed rumor the Americans had landed in North Africa.

They took the bridge across the Danube. The water below was oily and darkly whorled.

"Do you know something, Sophie? You've developed a new walk."

"A new walk?"

"Yes, you're swaying your hips."

117

"Am I? How funny." Seeing herself reflected in a shop window, she laughed out loud. "You're right. I hadn't noticed. Hans, can we be serious for a minute? I know it's not fair, with you just back, but we can't talk at home in front of the others. I've been thinking a lot about the pamphlets."

Somehow he always knew what she was going to say and still he was surprised. "So have I," he said.

"More people will listen to us now, with the war going badly."

"I wonder, Sophie. Have you ever heard of Helmut Huebener? He's done some pamphleteering in Hamburg."

"No. Do you think he'll join us?" she asked.

"Hardly. They guillotined him last month. He was seventeen."

"I see."

"And may I introduce Werner Steinbrink, a Berlin student? And Alfred Schmidt? Both free thinkers like yourself."

"I suppose you want to tell me they were executed, too."

"As a matter of fact they were, Sophie, and a good many others I could name have ended up in prison. We're finished with that business. You may not think I mean it, but I do. I'm not going to put your life in danger again. Besides," he added, forgetting that several excuses are less convincing than one, "it costs money to put out pamphlets." He wanted time to read a book, time to see his friends, to gossip and to laugh. He even wanted time for silence. He wanted to be left alone by Sophie, by the world, and by that second self which he could never quite put to sleep and which kept seeing nameless shapes floundering in the snow.

118

Sophie did not raise her voice or plead. She simply searched him with her eyes. "Eugen Grimminger would help with money if we asked him."

"I don't want Herr Grimminger's money. I simply want you alive, and me alive, and all my good friends alive . . . to a ripe old age. Honestly, Sophie, I've been off that train five minutes. I'd hoped for a family reunion, not an ambush."

"I'm sorry, Hans. When I get my teeth into something, I can't help leaving them there."

"False teeth, Sophie?"

"Don't laugh at me, Hans."

"It's almost Christmas, Sophie. Rejoice. The Scholl family is whole again. Be happy, please."

"Is happiness so indispensable to you, Hans?"

"Yes, dear, it is. Don't be angry with me."

"I'm not angry."

"Then smile; bring a little sunshine to this cold day." She did not lift her face. "I'll get you a new red dress for Christmas."

"I don't have any more ration coupons."

"I have. If you don't want a dress, I'll get you a hat, fiercely feathered, to make you feel safe. You know, when I get home, I'm going to soak in a tub up to here." He drew his finger in a line just below his nostrils. "And I'm not going to hurry. I'm going to soak until the water turns cold. And the first person who tries to get me out . . . well . . ."

"Gets her head lopped off," replied Sophie, going along with his mood.

"Right!"

They turned the corner and Hans covered the last few feet on the run. The door was flung open and his father was standing there. It was good to be home, and the bath water was as hot as he could take it. It was impossible to think of frozen armies, of traitors, of the dead in such a hot tub.

Finally Sophie knocked on the door. "Hans, if you haven't drowned, get out."

"Never!" He settled even deeper into the water. "Try and argue me into getting out."

But a whiff from the kitchen coming in under the door persuaded him. All his in-transit ration points were cooking there. Hans stepped out, letting Russia spiral down the drain. They ate well that evening. There was more food available than there had been a year before, and Hans ate until his eyes watered. They talked of old times and family memories, never of Russia, Hitler, or the war. Hans was happy to the point of tears and weary to the verge of collapse.

"Give me a hand, Sophie. Help me get this poor veteran up to bed," his father had said.

Hans had not resisted. "Don't wake me," he told them. "Not until the war's over, and maybe not even then." But he had wakened, the first time gasping in the dark from a dream full of dead bodies, and again toward morning when the room was full of sunlight.

That afternoon Hans had his inevitable tête-à-tête with his father amid the old dog-eared volumes in the library. It began awkwardly. His mother was there, a silent, aching presence, dusting the already dusted books.

"Were they decent to you in prison, Father?"

"Decent? Yes. After all, I'm here. But they frightened me." His wife looked at him with unhappy eyes. Herr Scholl put his arms gently around her. "*Liebchen,* trust me to say what is necessary to our son."

120

She tried to smile. "I'll leave you two men alone." Then she turned her pale face to Hans. "She's old," he thought. "Mother's old."

"Sometimes I'm not sure I know right from wrong anymore, Hans," his father said. "But it can't be wrong for a mother to want her family safe. She's had me to worry about. Must we both worry about you and Sophie as soon as you go to Munich?"

"Mother, there's a shelter right near our apartment, and we're always the first ones there when the alarm blows. You mustn't worry." Of course they had not been speaking of air raids, and though his mother left the room, Hans felt her presence in all that was said.

"Hans, I don't want you to think my opinions have changed," his father began. "But I have learned that prison is a fearful place. Those Gestapo people make death very real. When you reach my age, you're supposed to have some resignation. One ought not to mind a brush with death. But I do mind. I have never clung to each day so tenaciously. It must be even harder for a young man. Don't take risks, Hans. Expressing your opinions isn't worth it."

Hans walked along the shelves, touching the books. He was stunned. This from his father! And worse than his words was his manner; almost abject, it seemed to Hans.

"Father, what has Sophie been saying to you?"

"She's given me the impression that you have taken grave risks. There was a time when a German could act against these Nazis. My generation, not yours. It's too late now, and it frightens me to think that my old-fashioned standards have been planted in my children without the tempering effects of time. I don't want you to spend your lives for nothing. Believe me, these days you can face a man down with an argument that's overwhelming in terms of logic and humanity. And that man will agree with you and shake your hand. Then he'll turn you in to the Gestapo because, against all reason, Hitler is his god and he worships him. Or it may be for the opposite reason, because he fears him as he would the devil. You're enough of a realist to understand me. God knows, Sophie won't listen. I'm afraid for her. Whatever course you set for yourself, this war will end. Germany will lose. Have no doubt of that. But we are prisoners, Hans. That is our shame, but we can't change it. It's up to the Allies now. We can only wait patiently for peace and try to make amends for Germany. Peace is beautiful, Hans. Just to know that the knock at the front door at dawn is the milkman or someone with a special-delivery letter, not a man with a gun. It won't hurt you to say *Sieg Heil*. Make it a game, and remember, son, whatever you do, that responsibility extends beyond your own body. It's like a pebble thrown into a pool. The ripples travel far and wide."

Three days later, Hans and Sophie left for the winter term at Munich University. Their mother's eyes were misty when she took leave of them, and her nose was red in complete abdication of dignity. At the last moment she took Hans's hand in her own small dry ones as though she could not let him go. "Take care, *Liebling*," was all she said. Hans knew her family was the world for her. She would rather be the mother of the killer than the killed, if it came to that.

His father had said very little. "I hope you have learned something from my mistakes," were his last words.

Out of sight of the house, they walked briskly. Hans

pictured his parents still standing at the door. His father would turn away first, go to the library and hunch himself over a book. He would look vacantly at the pages for a while, and then he would begin to read. The Nazis had left him that. Mother would wash her hands. She would probably wash them a dozen times before the day was over. Yes, it was best to get away from so much concern before he was weakened by it.

"It will be good seeing Alex and Christl again," said Sophie, breaking into his thoughts.

"Very good," he replied. "By the way, I met Eugen Grimminger yesterday. We had a talk."

# CHAPTER NINE

● The interrogator rested wearily, with one hand braced against the cell wall. He gazed at the hand and seemed puzzled by the number of fingers he saw there. "Well, Scholl," he said finally, "we've spent some time together without achieving much clarity, but I do begin to understand the reason. You simply haven't matured to the point of understanding yourself, much less the world. You long-haired idealists,"—though Hans's hair was regulation army length—"you always go off half-cocked. Did you really think your pamphleteering would cause some sort of student revolt? Would end the war? I can't believe that. Surely you do not expect statues will be erected in your honor. Well, perhaps we'll talk again, Scholl. In the meantime, I have a cell mate for you. Helmut Fietz. Unlike yourself, a trivial person."

The prisoner was pushed inside as the interrogator departed. He carried two plates of food and muttered over his shoulder, "Tin-pot Mussolini!" Then he introduced himself and his crime. While standing on a beer barrel in a public place, he had compared Hitler to an assortment of farm animals. "Are you one of the Gestapo's temporary guests, like me?" he asked. "Or are you here for treatment? You know, the blindfold in the early morning." Hans didn't reply. "I'm sorry," said Fietz. "I shouldn't joke. Here, have your supper while it's hot. Say, what are you in for?" When Hans told him the charge, Fietz gave a long, low whistle. "I hope they don't torture you. Hear that screaming? Well, it's way down the corridor, but if you press your ear to the wall . . . Let me tell you, they're ingenious here. Nothing so grotesque as a whip, but I understand they like to paddle feet. They leave the shoes on so the feet can't expand or burst. If the shoes stand up, they can paddle for hours. Then they have those electrode things. You can expect that. They'll wheel in a portable generator with all sorts of wire coils and little metal clips. Look, you can see the strap marks on this bunk. They've used it here before."

"Were you planted to frighten me?" Hans asked. "If you were, you're doing a fine job."

"Say, I'm sorry if I've spoiled your supper. It's not half as bad as I'm making out. I just think you ought to be prepared, you know. I mean, it could be worse. One's fed here, and it's quite clean."

"It has roaches," said Hans dully. He had been trying to concentrate on the slow progress of a cockroach across the floor. "Must have dropped in from the window," Fietz said. He put his shoe on it and ground the shoe back and forth.

"I'm going to try and sleep," Hans told him. "That is, if you don't mind." He needed time to collect his resources, for the last hours were like a narrowing slot through which his thoughts could not pass. He lay back on the hinged board with its thin mattress roll and flung an arm across his face. Under closed lids, two red thumbs seemed to depress his eyeballs.

"Isn't this light barbarous?" His cell mate was irrepressible. "I hate an unshaded light bulb. Why don't they turn it off?"

"I suppose it's on account of me. So that I won't kill myself." Hans felt once more hopelessly to blame.

"Well, it can't be helped, then. If I were you, though, I'd try to sleep as much as I could. Even a man in prison is a free man when he's asleep."

After that there was merciful silence. Hans lay motionless on his hard bunk. His back began to ache, but after a while he slept soundly for the first time in prison. It was morning when he awakened refreshed. Somewhere a church bell was ringing.

There had been daylight at the high window for several hours when his cell mate was removed and a dark figure took his place. Hans's immediate reaction was fear. Then he realized it was Franz.

"May I talk to you, Hans?" Franz made his characteristic little gesture of uncertainty, like a Chinese shaking hands with himself.

"It's good of you to come, Franz. Or is this an official visit?"

"No, no. Not at all. We're alone. I give you my word. There's no one listening."

"I didn't really think so. Sit down, Franz."

"You look well, Hans, all things considered."

"Yes, I'm well enough. Franz, can you speak frankly?"

**127**

"Of course. Though, like it or not, we are enemies now, Hans."

"Is it Sunday, Franz?"

"Yes, it's Sunday."

"Is there a chance I can see my family tomorrow?"

"You will, Hans, if they're allowed in the courtroom. Your trial is tomorrow."

"I see." The sand was running faster than he had supposed. "Franz, it's very hard not knowing anything about Sophie. Please, if you've heard anything, tell me."

"She's too much like you, Hans, for her own good. Because she is a girl, they tried to give her a chance. They suggested that if she had understood, she wouldn't have involved herself in his affair. I saw the stenographer's notes, saw what she told them. 'It's you, not I, who have the wrong outlook,' she said. When they interrogated her, all she did was predict an Allied invasion in April."

"I knew it!" Hans tried to smile, but his face was trembling.

"She keeps demanding the same treatment as you, Hans. She worships you, you know."

"And Christl . . . can you tell me anything about him?"

"He's here, too."

"But how is he?"

"Despondent. You know what he's like. His wife just had a baby; she's not well. I think he'll plead insanity at the trial."

"I hope it does him some good."

"And you, Hans? Why don't you do the same?"

"I can't, Franz."

"I don't understand you, Hans. You baffle me. Once we

128

were friends, and look how it's worked out. It's like a bad dream, with the two of us here in this place, on different sides. And you won't even try to make things easier for yourself."

"I think what we did was right, Franz. Sophie knows it was. I won't humiliate myself for the privilege of dying by a doctor's needle. It isn't that much easier, is it?"

"Surely, Hans, you must see how wrong you are. Can you hear the voices of students outside clamoring for your release? No, because they're in their classrooms. They've forgotten you, because people don't really want liberty. They flee from freedom like children. They need guidance; they want to be told."

"I haven't the strength to argue with you, Franz."

"I'm not arguing," Franz replied. "I'm trying to save your life. Tomorrow you're to have a trial. As matters stand, it will only be a show, a formality to discredit you publicly and justify the sentence. The state prefers punishment to follow right after the trial. The same day, if possible."

"The way dogs are trained."

"Joke if you like, Hans. But I've seen the prisoners at Stadelheim, where they're taken after trial. I've seen the condemned in their last moments with their hands bound and their collars cut away. I've studied their faces when they first notice the blade above and the wicker basket below. There's no scaffold, Hans; no ascent out of this world. A guillotine's a plain and simple machine with nothing exalted about it. It's the logical solution to political divergencies. Picture this. The condemned is strapped to a tilting board. His face is as white as writing paper. He has played at being a hero or a saint,

**129**

he's come from court full of moral victory, but then at the last his body's fear drags him from his fool's paradise. Always. But by then it's too late. Yet he must go through with it, you understand. He never faints. You would expect it, at this point, with his head fixed now so he can scarcely turn it. I imagine his brain must be exceptionally active, thinking at a furious rate, knowing, and hearing above him the clang of the steel."

Hans forced his mind to digest every word. It was his own execution, and in a way it seemed that if he could endure it now, he would exorcize the reality to come. Only his body rebelled. His legs were numb and his stomach sent a hard bubble up into his throat, where it expanded, bringing a metallic taste into his mouth.

"It lasts only a fraction of a second, but he must surely hear it. Then annihilation. The blade is extremely heavy, you know. It takes the head off very close to the chin, but the body looks as though there were nothing left on the shoulders. Imagine! And imagine this. What if for one second the eyes see . . . or the head, looking up from the basket, knows that it has been severed. Think of that. Could it, Hans, for a second? Perhaps a minute? Just imagine!"

"All right. All right," Hans whispered. "I've imagined it all." He swallowed hard. "I want my life, Franz. If only I could find the way."

"Plead insanity, then. It's the surest way. Believe me, Hans, I'm on your side. We've been close friends, and I owe you a good deal, so let me speak frankly. They have against all three of you what a lawyer would call a prima-facie case of treason. If nothing is done to alter that, you will be dead within forty-eight hours. Do you hate life

130

that much, Hans? I can imagine dying after accomplishing something. But before? You must agree that's a waste."

It was love of life that had brought Hans to this cell. That was one thing he was sure of. A doctor had to love life and hate death. If he had not known this simple law before, he had learned it well in September of 1940.

Most of the medical students had returned from the victorious campaign in France. "Sailing Against England," a popular tune throughout August, was not being whistled anymore when Hans received his travel orders. He was to accompany a hospital train back to Frankfurt, take part in the disposal of the patients, and then proceed to Munich and the continuance of his medical studies.

Before dawn one morning Hans found himself embarking ambulatory patients onto a chain of passenger coaches haphazardly marked in whitewash with the medical cross. Methodically he assisted the wounded aboard, responding to the cold, damp impact of their hands with words of reassurance. Nothing, thought Hans, could have been more depressing for these ravaged men than the stained upholstery that conspicuously had borne wounded before. Each time he returned to the platform he would let out a long-contained breath with an explosive sigh before enduring another lungful of the sweetly fetid air.

Some leaned heavily on Hans as he tried to find them a seat, others resisted help angrily. "Damn it, I've got two legs," one man exclaimed. "I'll find my own place." The face was thinner, but gray no longer, the throat still bandaged, the left arm gone above the elbow. Full of sudden recognition, Hans pursued him. "I tell you I can cope! What are you staring at? There're plenty like me."

131

"Look here, soldier. You were strafed by a plane about two months ago, weren't you? Haven't you a blond sweetheart with enormous blue eyes?"

"You! You're the medic who kept me alive!"

Embarrassed by the obvious gratitude, Hans said, "Well, I told you you'd be going home, didn't I?"

"But you didn't believe it."

"Not then, I didn't," Hans admitted with a laugh.

The man threw a fond arm around Hans's shoulder. "I should have recognized you right off, but I didn't until I heard your voice. I'll never forget your voice. Your face, you know . . . it was just a balloon floating in the sky. Are you going home, too?"

Before Hans left to look after other casualties, the man insisted he return. "I'm saving this seat," he said.

The train made good speed. By the time Hans was able to sit down, they had entered Germany. The train roared along through the early dusk, a worm with a fiery head.

"Couldn't you use a decent night's sleep?" Hans asked the soldier, whose name, he had learned, was Felix.

"The modern sandman and his sleeping pills," Felix chided him "No, I'm fine. If you're tired, gobble your own pills."

Hans was tired, but he had a special interest in this man, whose life in a way belonged to him. "Look, there, now," he pointed. "You can see the Rhine."

"It's been a long time," said Felix. "Too long. When I get back home and cleaned up, I'm going to put on a checked jacket and a necktie with a chorus girl in flames painted on it. I'll look like an American gangster before I'll look like a soldier again."

"I don't understand why you weren't shipped back weeks ago."

132

"I was about to be, then, wham! Had a hemorrhage from this place in my throat. Nearly died. Damned cheerful doctor couldn't stop the blood, and the nurse was worse. She began telling me I'd be with my mother and father in the other world. They were a pair. I wanted to say, "To hell with you two morticians," but I didn't have the strength."

"Calm down. You've made it. You lead a charmed life."

"Still, it happened. And I could hemorrhage again, couldn't I?"

"I'm not a doctor yet," Hans admitted, "but I suppose it could happen. Not likely, though. I could fall off this train, but I'm not planning on it. Just take care of yourself." He went on to explain about secondary hemorrhages that occasionally occurred when the silk threads used to bind damaged vessels rotted away and were cast off by the growth of new tissue. There was the possibility of excessive activity moving a fragment of foreign matter not extracted by surgery.

"That's enough," Felix interrupted. "Here. Let me show you something nice." He produced a wallet and fumbled it open to a picture.

"Pretty," Hans remarked. "Very."

Felix smiled. "My wife. Such eyes. As though everything she sees is a surprise. This arm of mine won't put her off. Not my Heidi." He sounded as though he needed convincing, and his face for a fleeting instant looked afraid.

"What else have we got here?" Hans asked to distract him.

There was a card naming Felix as a founding member of the weight lifter's association of Totenberg. This he stuck between his teeth, tearing it with his one hand. "So much for that," he said. Then there was a photo of Felix with two nurses and another patient in front of the Eiffel Tower. Their uniforms were rumpled, and the nurses looked tired. The tower scarcely showed in the picture.

There was a night storm moving down the Rhine when the train stopped joltingly at the Remagen station. A station agent was pushing a wagon that bore a large yellow box used for transporting coffins. The rain and the wind struck together as if they had burst through something solid, and the agent ran for cover, leaving the wagon outside the train window. Heavy drops drummed like nails on the box. Presently the train moved again, swinging abruptly left and onto the Ludendorff railroad bridge. Built in 1916 for the advancing German army, it had two years later felt the weight of the first American occupation troops. It was a bridge with a past.

Outside the storm passed downriver, but the sky was heavy and full of echoes. Haystacks flashed by like men in raincoats.

Two hours later they were in the smoky suburbs of Frankfurt. A caravan of ambulances moved the patients to the hospital. Rubber-wheeled chairs made no noise on polished floors. Neatly spaced steel beds could be rolled silently on black rubber casters. To Hans, it seemed a place where no one would ever die from accident or neglect.

The days he spent working at the Frankfurt hospital before departing for Munich were crowded ones for Hans, but he checked up on Felix whenever he could. "I don't know why she wasn't here waiting," Felix told him the first evening. "She's not like my damned mother." Hans gave him a shot to make him sleep, but when his wife did not appear the second day, Felix became really agitated. "She'll come; don't worry," Hans assured him. "Listen, you'll postpone your discharge if you keep this up. Your blood pressure's way up, so take it easy. Civilians have trouble with transportation these days. She'll get here."

"She's got to, said Felix. "She isn't like my mother."

But it was a week before Heidi arrived. Hans was taking temperatures in Felix's ward when they first saw her. Felix told Hans later he had really given up all hope. At first he didn't recognize her, the details of her face. Then he wanted to run, to save the reunion for another time, when he had prepared himself. But the girl stood in the only exit, so he sat on the edge of his cot and pulled the blanket about his shoulders and his missing arm. By now she had noticed him and waved, her hand hesitating midway, as though she shared his reluctance. Very pale, her heels clipping icily, she walked straight to him and kissed him on the mouth. Her eyes did not really move toward the absent arm. She had some homemade cookies, neatly wrapped, and some magazines which she thrust at him in a bunch. She seemed unhappy that she had not brought more. Tiny pearls of moisture had broken out on her upper lip and on her forehead. She shifted from foot to foot. She could not find a comfortable place for her hands, for her two arms.

"Have they taken good care of you, Felix?" she managed.

"It's a very efficient hospital."

"I'm glad of that. I've been so worried." Her words tumbled together. There was another painful pause. "I saw your cousin, Frederika. She sends her best."

135

"She wrote me a letter."

"I know." His wife's eyes were fixed on the window and the brick wall beyond. "Have they fed you well?"

Felix had opened his heart, his hopes and his fears to Hans and to any nurse or patient who would listen. Now he could not speak to his wife.

"The meals here would make a pig vomit," he told her.

"Oh," she replied, still staring at the wall across the courtyard. "I made you some little cakes. In the package."

"*Liebchen*," he whispered, "a plane bit off my arm."

The girl swayed as though the ward floor were a shifting deck.

"Sit down, Heidi." Hans pushed up a chair. She looked at him and tried to smile. Then a patient in a nearby bed screamed for a doctor, and she said in a tone that echoed the agony and pain, "O, God! O, God!" As if for protection, she stepped nearer to Felix, and he caught hold of her hand.

"I want you to meet Hans Scholl," he said. "Not only did he save my life, but he is a very special member of the SS sent here to determine morale among the nurses."

"Please, that's classified," protested Hans.

"And he has made a certain number of findings that will be disturbing to Herr Himmler. Yes. For instance, very few of the patients here die from bullet wounds. That is so. Most of us die from something the doctors call ghostly wounds."

"Ghostly wounds?"

"Yes. Do you know the hurt when you have lost someone more precious than all the world?"

His wife put her head on Felix's shoulder, threw her arms around him, and began to cry.

136

A week later Hans was relieved of duty. He took the local train to Munich and after months of silence wrote a letter to Sophie.

My Dear Sister,

Forgive me for writing so seldom. You may not believe it, but you are always in my thoughts. We were once so innocent, you and I. Stay innocent if you can. Before I went to France, I used to believe there was some pattern to living, some meaning to early dying. I don't believe in patterns now. I had a patient, Sophie. He should have died in France, but he didn't. He came home, seemed cured, was reunited with his wife and discharged. I saw them off, went back to work and didn't find out until two hours later that an old throat wound had hemorrhaged. He was dead on the sidewalk before help came. Why then? Why not in France, if it was meant to be? Well, I am more cynical now. I just believe in one thing, staying alive. Life is a fragile gift, Sophie, and no principles, however glorious, can justify sacrificing a thing so precious. Life. That's the whole answer. So take care of yourself, and let me know when you will begin your studies in Munich.

Your fond brother, Hans.

If life had seemed precious then, and death an outrage, the feeling would later be magnified from the perspective of a field hospital in Russia.

It was there Hans wrote a long letter to Professor Huber, whom he had met through Sophie in the spring of 1942. Though the professor was worshiped by the University's liberal students, he and Hans had had one quarrel. Both favored the overthrow of the Nazi party, but Huber still believed in a special destiny for Germany, and he saw the army as an instrument of the Fatherland's fate. Just before Hans departed with the medical troop for Russia, he had said to Huber, "Will you object if I send you a letter or two this summer? I'll put your glorious army on the operating table."

"I'd be delighted," Huber told him. "I'm confident in your surgery."

During the first weeks at the front there was little to write about. Then, during the weeks of offensive and counteroffensive, there was no opportunity. Not until the October days of mud and exhaustion did Hans find time for the letter he had intended.

Dear Professor Huber,

The last time I saw you I promised to write, and now at last I will try to give you a medic's-eye view of your glorious army in the field. When I first arrived, we were not busy here. No fighting, merely the usual inglorious afflictions: rashes, scabies, lice, diarrhea. We could eat our meals off the operating table then. Sometimes we did, with Major Kramer dishing out the rations. He is our surgeon, too old, I think, for promotion, and too conscientious to seek discharge. I have never seen an uglier man. Huge, hairy nostrils and a big furry mole under his right eye, like the top of a bulrush. He is not in the least glorious, but I think you would admire him as

138

much as we all do. According to Major Kramer, only once in a millennium does a corporal become a great commander, and Napoleon has been dead only 120 years. One strike against the glorious army!

Roar of artillery one morning, and we haven't eaten off the operating table since. It all started with a terrific barrage. We just looked at one another. "So now they're getting down to work again," the Major said. He likes to talk of the field surgery as a human repair shop, and he had extra signs chalked up to direct the ambulances. "The conveyer belt from the front," he calls them.

We barely had time to lay out the freshly sterilized instruments and help the Major on with his gloves when the wounded began to arrive. My first job was to cut off their clothing and their boots. We're supposed to save the boots, if possible. What do you say to a man when you're cutting off his clothes and he's looking up at you with helpless suspicion? The Major always asks them their age and where they're from. He has such a confidential way. It seems to help. "Any broken crockery inside here?" he'll say. "Let's have a look." Sometimes, if they're not too badly off, he'll ask them about the battle. A field surgery must always know if the front's collapsing in order to clear out. So far we've only moved forward, inch by inch.

The wounded come in as long as there is fighting, and sometimes it goes on day after day. There are a few Russian planes, but they come over at night, so the operating theater is sealed up after dark with blankets. It smells horrible. Blood, sweat, alcohol and ether all together. It smells better during the day, but it's more melancholy. The red sun seems to press right through the canvas.

I don't think I can tell you what it's like to be a field surgeon, working 24 hours and longer at a stretch. I can't really appreciate it myself, nor can I imagine what goes on inside the Major, behind his bloodstained rubber apron and his white mask. I only know he never seems to tire and never loses his calm, even when the shells are falling very close. He simply lays down his scalpel with the whine of each shell and picks it up again after the concussion. When they are particularly close, we get down on the floor and the Major holds his gloved hands up over his head to keep them clean.

One gets used to the shelling, but I don't think I will ever get used to the wounded. The indignities we perform on their poor bodies. When I first assisted at the operations, I wasn't much help to the Major. If he put something into a basin, I couldn't look at it. I couldn't look at the patient's face. "Come alive, Scholl," the Major would say. "There are stitches to put in."

Well, I'm more hard-boiled than I used to be. I'm more useful, too. Let me tell you, one has to serve in a field surgery for a while to imagine the infinite number of ways a human body can be mutilated. Rifle bullets are the only things that leave a neat, straight wound. Sometimes they make blue and bloodless marks like knots in a tree. But very few men are hit that way. Usually it is the ragged fragment of a mortar shell laying open the secret life

140

of a chest or a stomach. What a bright array of colors inside the human body, like a palette covered with fresh squiggles of oil paint. With a head wound there is little we can do but ship them back to the base hospital. We have no diagnostic equipment. With a wound in the abdomen, there's hope within two hours or so. After twelve hours there doesn't seem to be a chance. That's why our Major never stops. The rest of us are dropping from fatigue, and he goes on. Sometimes I hold a cigarette for him in a surgical clip, or help him drink coffee without his touching the cup. There is something invincible about the man, but also something pitiful. He seems to be trying to undo the work of every shot fired in battle. He can't, of course. Many die here, though many are saved.

Our struggle doesn't end at the operating table. Sometimes the wounded aren't sent back to the rear for days. One changes bandages, tries to console the suffering. This is hardest of all for me. A wounded man cries, particularly at night, not from pain, but for the ruin of his body. How many ways are there to cry? Mechanically, like a trapped rabbit; like a gnat in a bottle; like a sad old crippled owl in the forest; like a child who wants his mother. Not all cry. Some can't. They just breathe too fast, like a cracked bellows. Others don't seem to know what has happened to them. The shock of being badly hit is a kind of anesthesia, you know. The average man is angry and incredulous about being helpless. For him, we try to make it seem amusing. A man has his skull split open and we tell him, "No one dies from a sinus headache." I remember one poor devil who had lost his arm on the battlefield. That didn't seem to bother him, but we couldn't get him to stop crying because of the wristwatch he'd been wearing—some sort of heirloom. Well, eventually they leave us to become someone else's problem. "Send me a card from Berlin, you lucky dog." That's what I usually say to them, and I don't believe I've ever called anyone a lucky dog before.

I am no magician like the Major when it comes to bedside chatter, but I've learned to manage as well as most. No amount of practice will ever teach me what to say to a man who is mortally injured. Not that one can always tell. Some die rapidly from tiny wounds you would not expect to kill a mouse. Others are like snakes: bones broken, heads laid open, intestines spilling out like so much spaghetti, but they take day after day to die. More often than not, the patient seems to know. A man dying in a field surgery, a man in his prime with most of life unfulfilled—believe me, his anguish is boundless, and any efforts to console him are pitifully meager. Do you tell him he will be buried like a hero, lie in holy German soil? He won't. Can you tell him he has died for a better world? He hasn't. To keep his wife safe? They all know about the air raids back home. I am no stranger to deathbeds now, but I've found there is no honest vocabulary for such occasions.

Let me tell you about a boy we had here last week. He had wounded himself deliberately. There are quite a few like that. You can tell by the powder burns, even though the Russians drop leaflets telling them how to mutilate themselves undetectably. We're supposed to report these cases, you know, for disciplinary action. In any case, with this one it didn't matter. He'd let it go too long and had gangrene that was out of control. What a smell! Anywhere near him, you had to breathe through your teeth. Still, wc pretended he was going home. I gave him morphine as if it would make him well. Still, he knew, so I tried to help him pray. He told me not to bother. "Don't you believe in prayer at all?" I asked him, and he told me, "No!" "Did you ever believe?" And he answered, "Once, when I believed in giants, too." For him there was no heaven or hell, it was life or nothing. He wouldn't consent to die. He fought for life like a tiger. Even when one leg was off and the other had been dead for days, the rest of him refused to die. I sat beside him that last night under a pool of lamplight. The light was within a few feet of his eyes, but he thought I'd put it out. "Oh, you know the blackout regulations," I told him, and gave him more morphine. At the very last he must have mistaken the approach of death for the return of health, for he whispered, "I'm better now." At least I shall envy him that when my time comes. "A waste of morphine," one of the medics said, a sad but I'm afraid accurate, requiem. Who was he? We didn't even know his name, and now I didn't want to. He was dead; small and flat and, yes, revolting. Death is revolting. Their dying makes my hands sweat still. I have worn a shiny patch on my trousers from seeing so many die.

Day after day a jumble of heads and legs and arms. Perhaps famous statesmen of the future cut down. No matter, it is quicker to bury them in compost than in marble, and until recently the weather has been warm. If we do not bury them fast enough, they change every day in appearance, turning from yellow to black, and swelling enormously.

Unlike the stars, there are many anonymous soldiers. I stood watching a burial party the other day, wondering how it made the freshly wounded feel. We'd just gotten a mob through surgery, and I was tired. Anyway, the Major came up and asked me how I felt. "Sick," I told him. "You have to be alive to feel sick," he said. Well, I felt ashamed. "Why does it have to go on?" I asked him. You know, the child wanting the last word. "Well," he said, sounding very matter-of-fact, "there are over twelve million German boys in the field. They are the manure of history preparing the ground with their bodies for national greatness." At first I was afraid he meant it. But then he said, "You know I don't believe that sort of Party claptrap. But we must continue to fight now because we can no longer afford to lose."

"Do you think we can win?" I asked him. He said, "No. Only the undertakers can win, but it will be a bad war to lose." "You mean to be overrun by the Russians would be worse than death?" This made him laugh. "You ought to know better than that, Scholl. Nothing's worse than death." I could get no more out of him.

I have heard that the front line in autumn is a sea of mud. To me it seems more of an open cesspool.

But, I thank God, for the time being the guns are quiet and there is no mutilating. As you can see, I've time to write very long and disagreeable letters. What I've told you is what I've seen and done and what I can't put into a letter to Sophie. If you find it repulsive, so much the better. Regard it as a continuation of our standing argument. I have seen no glorious cavalry charges nor anything else that would make me speak in rhymed couplets of our great military tradition. But you were warned. I will write again when I have the chance. In any case, if I'm lucky, I will be home from this crusade in late autumn and we can argue face to face.

Major Kramer censored the letter himself. "I found it very interesting, Hans," he said. "I'm sorry I had to cut so much. But you won't end the war with this sort of thing, and you could get into trouble. We don't want the SS nosing about, do we?" So a few tattered fragments were posted to the professor two weeks before Hans himself left Russia with the coming of the first heavy snow.

# CHAPTER TEN

● "Come back, Hans." Franz shook his shoulder gently. "Come back from Russia and listen to me. You're in a Gestapo prison cell, remember; but out that barred window, if you could see beyond the brick walls, you would see the Alps, Hans. I saw them this morning as I drove here. They were snow-capped, glistening. You used to say you could spend your life in the mountains, and believe me, soldiers are there right now, skiing, hiking with their girl friends, having a fine time. They will be there tomorrow and the day after. Then I parked near the cemetery down the block, all trampled and muddy. People are there, too, forever. You still may choose between them, but you have very little time."

"Don't mistake me, Franz. I don't want to die or spend my life in a cell. If I can only find an honest way out."

"Good. I knew you'd agree, Hans. That's why I'm here. Rid yourself of all doubts. I'm no spy. I'm here as your friend. I owe you a great deal. That time with the chickens, and when you fought Otto over the flag. I've never forgotten that. And then there was that trouble with Father. You remember that."

Hans would never forget it.

It had been a hot mid-summer night in 1934. All the windows were open, so that he heard them long before they rattled at the door. Franz had burst in, pale and breathless.

"Hitler, Goering, that Himmler fellow . . . oh, God, Hans!"

Then Herr Bittner had pushed in behind his son. He looked diminished and furtive. "They're after me," he said. "Is your father here, Hans?"

"No, sir. He's in Munich on business. What's going on? Can I help?"

"You know Rolf Bittner, same name as mine?"

"Yes, the grocer."

"He's dead . . . just now . . . murdered by the SS."

"But why?"

As the story unraveled, with Franz and Herr Bittner interrupting one another, it seemed that the Storm Troopers had grown too independent and strong under Ernst Roehm, head of the SA. A purge was underway. Hundreds were being shot. Roehm had already been disposed of, and Herr Bittner, as his staunch supporter, was certainly marked for death. The murdered grocer had been mistaken for him.

"I'll do what I can," Hans promised.

That night he hid them in the shed that often harbored Sophie's hurt animals. The next morning he brought them food and hiking gear from the storeroom. He could think of only one way, to make for the Swiss border through the Alps. Hans had climbed there often, but the first part of the journey had to be made by train. This became a nightmare of suspense. Herr Bittner's head roved constantly from side to side, one hand under his jacket clutching what was certainly a pistol, while SS prowled through the cars. It was easier once they started hiking. Hans tossed aside the sounds and smells of civilization with rolling shoulders and loose-jointed strides. Even the Bittners appeared more relaxed, though they were less accustomed to climbing.

They had followed the river paths upward, passing horse-drawn timber wagons and frowning monasteries until the Lattenburg loomed before them. Beyond were the mists of Sonntagshorn, and the bigger mountains, Hochkalter and Leongänger Steinberg. Still further wrapped in pearl-white mystery, lay the Swiss and Austrian Alps.

They had climbed until dusk. "I'm finished," Herr Bittner kept saying. "They'll keep after me. I can't get away from them." He saw the glitter of knives in every tree, and imagined pistols being aimed at him from every stone and bush.

Hans had almost been able to forget Herr Bittner on the climb. The mountains seemed to grow taller as they ascended. The last range of trees gave way to bare slopes and natural battlements that merged with the cloudy palaces of heaven—a majesty beyond words. Surely there were no enemies beyond the mountain itself. Where scrub pines stood against the sky and the sun dappled a pine-needled floor, they pitched a small tent and camped. "We'll get there tomorrow," Hans promised. "Meanwhile, I'm for a good meal and a good night's sleep."

Somewhere a storm growled and tricks of wind worked the triangular tent openings filling it with irregular splashes of white light.

"Now it will thunder," Franz had said.

149

"Far away." Hans kept tying the flaps together, but Herr Bittner would open them and prowl outside.

"I used to be afraid of thunder," Franz said. "Father, remember how you used to wake up yelling your head off in a thunderstorm?" Bittner stared vacantly at his son. "In his sleep, he'd think it was a British attack. He thought he was back in the trenches."

Outside, rain began to drum down. A melody of deep beating chords like racing footsteps seemed about to burst open the flaps.

Hans took the charred meat from the spit, pressed a loaf of bread against his chest and sawed it apart. The fresh dark dough stuck to the blade. He scooped butter out of a small crock with his fingers, then passed the food along. Herr Bittner's hands were trembling when he took his portion.

"Father," Franz said as if recalling a joke, "remember our games with tin soldiers? Hans, he always won. Don't you remember, Father, how you'd flatten my poor fellows? I had a little tin corporal in my army. One day I painted on the tiniest red arm band and black moustache, so small you'd never notice it. You never noticed it, did you, Father?"

What was Franz up to? Hans wondered. In the green-whiteness of a lightning flash, he saw that the boy was scowling, his mouth hard set. His father kept squirming around, kneading his hands together. What was going on? Herr Bittner had seemed reasonable enough in the mad world of Nazi Germany, but as they moved further into the mountains, his every action seemed increasingly unbalanced.

"Do you recall, Father, how we used to march our armies

across the floor, step by step, step by step? Creeping up on each other? If I'd painted my men black like the SS, Father, you'd never have seen them creeping up, getting closer all the time. You know, Hans, my father has always had the utmost respect for the SS and Herr Himmler. You should meet Herr Himmler, Hans. He's very impressive. Can you imagine one of those great bird-catching spiders from the Amazon translated into human terms and endowed with intelligence little less than human? If you can imagine such a creature spinning its web very quickly and thoroughly . . ." Never once did Herr Bittner interrupt his son, but he swung his gun forward in its holster and unfastened the button that retained it.

Outside the lightning darted along the ground. Strokes of thunder hung in the air, more felt than heard. Then, without warning, as though to catch an intruder off guard, Herr Bittner lunged at the tent flaps and burst outside, his pistol aimed. He was not quick enough. No one was there.

He's thinking about gas," Franz explained. "He's been worried for a long time that the SS might push a rubber tube under his door and poison him with gas at night."

"It's not very likely in a tent," Hans said. It was all so insane, he fought down a desire to laugh.

"Well, they could do it with a portable tank. They could slip a hose in here while we're asleep."

If Herr Bittner listened, again he said nothing. His face seemed frozen by fear.

"I wouldn't mind some sleep," said Franz. "All that sun and exercise, and more of the same tomorrow."

They were to leave at first light, up the laborious trail to Switzerland. The two boys would return, but Herr Bittner would seek political asylum. It was a prospect for which rest was essential, and Hans settled down to sleep. Only Herr Bittner sat crouched in the corner, apparently listening for the movement of a rubber tube and the first sibilant hiss of death.

As the tent was on elevated ground, the pine needles underneath remained dry and sweetly scented. Hans lay on his side, his hand over his face. He yawned and felt a warm glow creeping through his clothes. The blanket smelled of smoke and old camphor. He slid effortlessly into a dream of perfect happiness. Then suddenly he was starkly awake. Someone had screamed. In a glimmer of distant lightning, he saw Herr Bittner stiffen, saw his lips gnawing in fearful contortion, before he scuttled through the tent flaps, his pistol firing as he went. Hans heard him crash through thickets, then his feet scrabbling on loose shale, and then there was silence.

Hans expected the son to plunge after the father, but to his amazement Franz seemed very close to mirth.

"What happened?" Hans demanded.

"I don't know whether to laugh or cry," replied Franz. "Look at this." He held up a round black stick shiny with wetness. "It was jammed under the edge of the tent, just like a rubber hose."

Hans laughed without wanting to. "Franz," he managed, "Franz, I'm sorry. I'm not a sadist, honestly. It's just the tension of yesterday, and now this. Don't worry. We'll find him."

"That's all right," Franz said. "It is funny. He's off to the twilight land, my father. The land of the daft. And there's not a thing we can do about it till morning."

In the blackness and the storm, Hans knew that, of

152

course, Franz was right. He called Herr Bittner's name several times, but the only answer was the rolling thunder. Sleep was out of the question, and with the first dull light of morning they left the tent.

It was not long until they found him, lying flat on his back, mouth and eyes agape with the terror that had killed him. They stood and stared until Franz said softly, "The ultimate flight—my father from himself."

"Suicide?" asked Hans.

"Not Father."

The gun was still in the dead man's hand. There was no evident wound, and clearly he had not fallen.

"His heart must have given out," Franz said. "He's had attacks before."

"My God, Franz! Then he shouldn't have been up here, climbing."

"What else was there to do?" Methodically Franz went through his father's pockets. "Good. Here's the money and his papers."

"Shall we rig up a sling and carry him down?"

Franz said, "Hans, will you come with me?"

"Where do you think I'm going? Besides, you can't carry him alone."

"Not with him," Franz explained. "I mean to Switzerland. I haven't the guts to go alone, but if you'd come . . . Look at all this money. I'd divide it with you. We could eat a lot of fondu, Hans."

Hans was speechless. A man lay dead at his feet while his son talked calmly of eating cheese and starting a new life in a foreign land. A new life . . . there was a strong appeal in the idea of having done with Hitler. It would have been simple to slip away, but Hans loved his family,

**153**

and his roots were deep. Franz must have read the answer in his face, for he did not repeat his question.

"What do you want done with your father, Franz?"

"What is there to do? Let him lie there. He's not like a tin soldier. No use setting him up again; he'll just fall down."

"We can't just leave him."

"Why not? It's perfectly easy. Look, I'm going to write a suicide note in case he's found. I'm not joking. It's the best thing for me. For Mother, too. It will be a very heroic document. All about how he realized that he'd sinned against the Party and stood in the way of progress. That sort of nonsense."

Franz was not joking. It was as though he had envisioned the scene before. He began to write on an envelope. Hans felt strongly that they should carry Herr Bittner home, but it would be an ugly job at best, and one that would involve them in nasty investigations. Then, too, the decision belonged to Franz. The note finished, Franz was all business. He inserted it into his father's breast pocket.

"There, " he said. "Now I'd better make this seem like suicide. Would you rather not look?" But Hans could not help staring while Franz reloaded the pistol. He forced the gun into his father's stiffening hand, managed to work it around so that the muzzle fitted crookedly into his father's open mouth. As Franz manipulated the cold finger, Hans turned away.

The shot was muffled. Even the birds went on singing.

After a silent breakfast they started down the mountain together, still not communicating. By afternoon, they had descended into a world full of rumor and report. The SA had been wiped out; hundreds of them. They had been plotting to overthrow the government, so it was what they deserved, according to the official reports.

Once again it was Franz's hand on his shoulder that brought Hans back to the present, the cell, his weariness.

"You're exhausted, Hans. I ought to leave you to get some sleep. I could get you a sedative," Franz offered.

"No, no thanks. I'm all right. We were talking about the time in 1934 with your father."

"Yes, it was the last week end in June," Franz said. "I don't think we really saw each other again until the war."

"In the railroad station, once or twice."

"And then that time with Sophie on the train. Remember that?" Franz asked.

"Very well," Hans admitted, as a whole new set of memories came flooding back.

It had been the late, full-blooming spring of 1942. The campaign in France was a fading memory, the summer in Russia an imminent prospect, and as a last gesture before leaving for the Eastern Front he and Sophie had taken their suitcases loaded with leaflets to the Munich station. Hans remembered feeling the cold eyes of suspicion upon them. The buildings seemed to lean over them as they went by; as they turned the corners, a watcher slid from sight, though he had no shape or name.

The station itself had been full of Nazi officials. Ordinary citizens were lucky to find standing room on the infrequent trains. In that crowd, with the suitcase slapping at his side, Hans felt like a spy in a foreign land who had been taught the customs and the native language.

They had bought their tickets and were about to board

the Ulm train when one of the black uniforms detached itself from the others and moved toward them with a purposeful booted stride. The air of withered youth, the red, irritated complexion was immediately recognized by Hans. He set down the suitcase and held out his hand. "Franz!"

Heels clicking together, Franz kissed Sophie's hand, a gallantry never before observed. She greeted him in a voice that was calm and quiet, too calm and quiet even for Sophie.

Franz startled them both by saying, "I suspect I'm not altogether welcome here."

"Come now, an old friend like you, Franz?"

"Yes, of course." He produced a loud cough of laughter.

Franz, it turned out, was taking the same train, and he insisted upon carrying Sophie's bag. "Going home?" he asked.

"Just for the week end," Hans replied.

"This certainly is good luck." Hans and Sophie pronounced all the proper clichés, like well-meaning actors who try their best but who are basically without talent. They would have preferred locating themselves as far as possible from their dangerous luggage, but Franz found them all seats and shoved Sophie's bag beneath his feet.

He had been promoted, he said. His transfer to Stadelheim Prison should arrive any day. Clearly life was treating him as he felt it should. The neglected boy had grown at last into a uniform that made men who were not afraid of God afraid of him. "And if I've been lucky, I owe a lot of it to you and my father, God rest his soul," he said. "Do you know that when they found my father's body, he became a Party martyr? Why, for a time "The

156

Bittner Lament" rivaled "The Horst Wessel Song." At least in Ulm. Did you ever hear it, Sophie?"

"Once or twice," Sophie admitted.

"Naturally they couldn't do enough for the son of a Party hero. I wouldn't otherwise be where I am today. And what about your plans, Hans? . . . Russia, eh?" he said thoughtfully after Hans had explained. "I never envy a man in Russia. Did I tell you Otto's there?" After the anticipated capture of Stalingrad, Otto would be moving in with the Action Group SS to purify the place. "Nasty business, race purification. This is in strictest confidence, but I've never been able to swallow the race theories. Actually, I'm against all killing of human beings, and that even includes Jews. Sterilization, maybe, but not some of the things I've seen. The roundups, the arrests . . . I don't know. It's hard to dispute that as long as so many good Germans must die for the nation, then why not the Jews as well? If the official point of view were only clarified— that we fight not for liberty, but for something much more important in the long run—human perfection—it would all be so much easier. Certainly, Hans, you can understand how practical it would be to look at things that way."

Hans had understood nothing. He had not really listened. Instead he had been watching the nervous wanderings of Franz's left hand as one might watch the ramblings of a scorpion. The long fingers had moved across his chest and down as if to fasten on Sophie's knee, but in fact had found their way absently to the latch on her suitcase. There they played with the first latch and worked it free.

"There really is so much misunderstanding of Party goals," said Franz. "Have you heard about the children throwing bricks at trains? It's becoming such a hazard, an

157

appeal has been put in the paper. Not that it's sabotage . . . only high spirits, surely. And this pamphleteering in town. That White Rose business. That's going too far, wouldn't you say?"

His hand, still wandering absently, had reached the second latch. Sophie jerked the bag toward her. "Well, Franz. Are you one of those weird types who like to handle girls' clothing?"

She spoke so sarcastically that Franz actually apologized. "Wandering fingers," he said hastily, adding to Hans, "What did you say you thought about the White Rose society?"

"I don't think I did say. Certainly they're taking an awful risk."

"Yes, that's true. A great risk." The pale eyes measured Hans. "What interests me is just how you feel about that sort of thing, Hans. Off the record, I know you've always fancied yourself a liberal. But Hans, at heart you're a German. What would you do to them, say, if they were caught and you were the judge? Off with their heads?"

Hans wasn't sure whether they were talking to while away the time or tapping out a verbal code. He only knew he felt like a victim of St. Vitus' Dance. It was just a matter of time before his muscles would begin to jerk.

"I can't deny I'm a pacifist. I don't believe in killing."

"Exactly, Hans. Mind you, this isn't the accepted view. As far as I'm concerned, these leaflets are therapeutic. You know, a harmless letting off of steam. Students need that sort of thing. Yes, it's believed to be students at the University who are behind it. Overlook it, is what I say. It's active physical rebellion one can't tolerate. For instance, that shocking tragedy in Poland, when Heydrick was assassinated last May. That's not to be endured, but capital

158

punishment must never become an indiscriminate thing or it loses its practicality." Whether this was simply an intellectual exercise, Hans could still not be sure. The saying that a person's eyes are the windows of his soul certainly did not apply to Franz. His pale-blue eyes were as secret as they had ever been.

"Sophie, it looks as if you may have to open your precious luggage after all," Franz said. Sophie sat up tall, straightening her back. "Don't bristle at me. I'm no fetishist. But it does seem odd, taking such heavy suitcases for a week end at home. I'm just trying to think like one of those fellows down at the end of the car. See them?" A pair of policemen had begun to search, a not uncommon practice due to black-market traffic.

Slowly the officials worked their way down the car. Sophie's face continued to express the most formidable calm. Hans hoped that he was equally impassive, but inside, his whole nervous system seemed to be separating itself from central control. He dared not speak lest his first word be a shriek. Soon his legs would refuse to obey him. Like a dreaming dog's, they would run of their own volition.

The police were nearer now, only one compartment away. Even if they did not intent to search, they would hear the hammering of his heart. When the request finally came, "Your luggage, please. Fräulein, will you open your luggage?" Hans felt himself screaming silently, as a trapped mole must scream deep in the earth.

Hans intervened his identification papers and the passport showing he was a member of the Munich Student's Company. "This is my sister," he told them in a precise, slow voice unmarked by any range of emphasis. "I'm sorry," said one of the officers. "This is entirely routine.

Fräulein, if you please . . ." If the clapper on the doomsday bell was about to swing, it was Franz who held it back. He identified himself. His awesome association was clear. These were his friends and he would appreciate it if the civil police would have some respect. Would a member of the Death's Head SS be in the company of black marketeers? And if he were, was it prudent for a member of the civil police to find it out? The policemen responded with skeptical grunts, and in the end they went their way. Franz sat back in his seat, the sole proprietor of the enigma he knew himself to be. "They are a nuisance," he said, clearly reveling in this display of power. "I would do a lot more for my oldest friend if you would permit me, Hans. I may call you my oldest friend, may I not?" Chronologically he had a right, no one could deny that. "I really never have had a good friend, Hans—one I could count on—except for you. I have never been a particularly attractive fellow." It took a certain courage to acknowledge such a merciless truth about oneself, but what about this allegation of friendship? Was Franz sincere, or was he using words as counters in an artful game?

Hans was not to find out. The train was already slowing. The station was Dachau. Once more Franz saluted Sophie's hand. As though prompted by some inner demon, he said, "I don't want you people getting involved in this White Rose affair. You're too good for that. Take care, now." Then he departed, taking his undecipherable face with him.

From the platform he waved once, then strode away.

"Hans, he knows! He knows everything! Sophie's eyes were wide.

"How can he? He can't possibly know."

"But you felt it, too. The things he said, Hans. The hints!"

160

"Yes, I felt it. But what does he intend? I can't judge him, Sophie. If he knows, why did he save us?"

"He's your friend, yet he seems so alien to me. And to you, too."

When the train finally moved, Hans gave a long whistling sigh of relief. They talked no more, but let the train lull the alarmed chemistry of their bodies. Sophie slumped in her seat, the fingers of both hands forming a protective grill before her face. Hans closed his eyes. He felt in that artificial darkness like a diver emerging from deeper, blacker depths.

"I did suspect you then, Hans. I suspected, and I tried to give you both a scare to warn you. There were leaflets in your baggage, weren't there? And you went right on with it."

"Yes, we went on with it," Hans admitted.

"And after you came back from Russia, you went right back to work again. You just changed the name from White Rose to "Leaflets from the Resistance." I suppose you thought that wouldn't seem so much a student affair. You know, Hans, I knew all along. Remember that Christmas party last winter?"

"Very well. That was a happy night," Hans said.

"For me, too."

But it had been happier before Franz arrived.

News from Russia had crept into the classrooms like sifting snow that Christmas season. Knots of conversation formed in the corridors between lectures. In the laboratories, where chemicals and fuel for the Bunsen burners ran low, there was whispering. At Stalingrad a German army was surrounded. El Alamain, and now this. Though the church bells sounded more of doom than Christmas, Hans took refuge in a season that had always been a time

**161**

of happy innocence for him. He and Sophie had always been the first among their childhood friends to try their sleds on the hill, the first to venture onto thin ice with their skates, and later, the most adventurous skiers. The shocks of war, the absence of familiar faces, inclined them to cling closer together. Hans made a tree from cardboard, and Sophie produced sweet biscuits and jam that she had hoarded for Christmas Eve.

Outside, Munich was sullen. The musicians and the snowmen fashioned into clowns were missing from the Karlsplatz, and in front of the City Hall no huge Christmas tree stood beneath the *Glockenspiel*. There were no colored lights in the city, no bands, and the marionette theater was closed. Hans had wanted to go home to Ulm, but the trains were packed with soldiers on leave and officials with priority. On Christmas Eve Hans shopped for Sophie's gift. He had told her emphatically, "No gifts," but he knew that she was knitting him a pair of socks. Another pair had already been presented to Alex. Ignoring the larger shops, where Saint Nicholas had greeted children with the Party salute, he visited the flower market, which became the Christkindlmarkt at this season. A few tents were set up, but none of the accustomed mounds of candies and cookies were for sale. An old market woman roasted chestnuts over a fire that would have to be extinguished with darkness. There was little to choose from, and when the decree closing all luxury shops went into effect on the first of the new year, there would be nothing. At one stand he found a simple secondhand music box. He hoped it would make Sophie happy. If it only made her nostalgic and a little sad, well, that was part of Christmas, too.

162

She was decorating the cardboard tree when he arrived.

"Look. I've almost finished," she said. "You put the star at the top. It's like faith . . . you must put it up high." Hans fixed the painted star in place. She mocked him gently. "I'm afraid it has six points, Hans. Is that dangerous? Do you think that's taking a risk?"

"What else did you do today?"

"Well, I ironed this dress."

"It looks fine. I should have said you look fine. You look radiant, Sophie. Are you expecting company?

"It's Christmas Eve, Hans. Alex may come."

"Outside, the snow's falling in great big holiday flakes. Sophie, look here. I've brought you a gift. It's not much; it's not even wrapped." The small wooden box played *O Tannenbaum* when Sophie raised the lid, and they listened spellbound until the spring wound down.

"If you could have absolutely anything for Christmas, Sophie, what would it be?"

"That's a silly game, Hans."

"A chalet way up in the mountains, full of crystal and candles?"

"I don't know."

"Or maybe a yacht sailing in the South Pacific?"

"Alex always said he wanted to sail around the world. He'd like that."

"No, something for you."

"Can it be very terrible?"

"Anything."

"Then I would like Herr Hitler's severed head to hang on the tree."

"Hush, Sophie!" He had a sudden apprehension of someone standing outside the door.

"Even Goebbel's wizened little skull . . . We could put a candle in his mouth." She paced up and down, talking loudly and recklessly.

Hans flung open the door to catch them there, but the corridor was empty. It was seeing Franz that afternoon, he supposed, that had made him so nervous. Franz in his black uniform; Franz who came and went from the execution jail at Perlacher, the place where traitors died.

"Hans, I'm an ungrateful wretch," Sophie said. "I should have said all I wanted was a music box. I do love it. But I can't be a hypocrite about this fake tree with its foolish little star." He told her to say anything she pleased as long as she said it softly.

"Hans, what's the matter with you?"

He was thinking of the block wardens with their squeaking dynamo flashlights. Any one of them who heard such talk would denounce them.

"What's that noise?" he asked.

"Only the wind under the door."

He put his hand to her mouth. Beyond the sound of the clock, the moan of the wind, there was something else, a faint sound of movement, quite close. This time there was no mistake. Someone was at the door. "Sophie," he whispered, "hide, quickly!"

"Hans, you're acting like a madman."

The doorknob rattled. Someone banged at the door.

"Gestapo," Hans whispered, but Sophie shook her hair back defiantly.

"Anybody home? Hans, merry Christmas!" It was Alex Schmorell.

Hans was relieved and irritated at the same time.

"I told you Alex was coming. Alex, come in."

164

"Ah, Sophie Magdelene Scholl! May I say you are a picture this evening?"

"A picture of what?"

"A picture that I like to look at carefully. A very classic study that makes me say, 'Good work, human race.'" Alex bestowed a regal kiss upon her hand and then they embraced warmly. It made Hans happy to see them together.

"You know, Sophie, I love you," said Alex.

"I know you love all females," she chided.

"I love them in you."

"If you love me, have you brought it?" she demanded.

"My new socks? Wonderfully warm. Splendid fit. Or do you mean Italian wine? Yes, one full bottle, and hard to get."

"You know what I mean. My special Christmas present."

"Me?" Alex said. "Is that what you want? If we get married tomorrow, will you be best man, Hans?"

"Absolutely." Hans wanted them to get married. They were his two favorite people. He thought Sophie wanted it, too.

She made a dive for Alex's jacket pocket. He pulled away. "Not yet, Sophie. It's Christmas, a time for peace and love." But still she pursued him. "Sophie, I appeal to you as a woman . . ."

"You know you do," she joked, still intent on extracting something from his pocket. "There!" Triumphantly she held up a captured bit of paper. "You did bring it."

The paper contained Alex's first effort at propaganda. Until now Hans had done all the writing, but they had agreed a change in style and emphasis might confuse Gestapo comparison with earlier leaflets.

They sat around the small table as Sophie read. Hans hunched forward, intent on every word. Alex lounged indolently, his legs flopped apart like those of a weary grasshopper.

Sophie read softly but with fervor. "Leaflets to the Resistance Movement . . . a call to all Germans!" She made it sound like poetry. "The war moves toward its inevitable end: defeat for the Nazi Party. The Nazis must be destroyed, not so much for spawning this terrible war, as for their unnatural crimes against our Jewish people. Untold thousands, perhaps millions, have been ruthlessly murdered. No crime in history can compare . . ." And so it went, voicing Alex's theme, one that went back to an Oktoberfest before the war and a young Jew named Saul. In this regard, they had often discussed what direction the leaflets should take. Alex favored attacking the Party only for its Jewish purge. At least in battle, he felt, every soldier had a sporting chance. For Hans, however, all war was unnatural and criminal. The soldier who died with a gun in his hands was as much the victim of unjustifiable murder as any other. Hans hated it all and refused to distinguish one death from another, but this was Alex's turn and he would not interfere. He hoped only that for a time they might put the Nazis from their minds, and think, however hypocritically, of Christmas.

When Sophie had finished reading, they sat quietly for some time. Snow hissed against the windows.

"I wish I could hear sleigh bells," Hans said. "There were always sleigh bells at home."

"When will we print it?" Sophie intruded. "We have time, with classes not in session."

166

"Not until day after tomorrow," Hans replied. "Let me have time to enjoy Christmas."

"So we three are playing games again," said Alex. "I'd bet on the odd or even number of mourners at a funeral—anything, so long as there's a fair chance, but I don't know about you, Hans. Deep down, I don't think you like gambling. It's not the game with you, it's the winning or losing. When you get nervous about the cards, you're apt to forget to hold them close to your chest."

"I've never liked games either," said Sophie. "But we're not playing games."

"If I didn't think we had a chance, I wouldn't be here, Sophie. Only a damned fool, like that Jew Saul, commits suicide, and falling into Gestapo hands would be a good deal worse than that. They'd see that we all talked. They'd press cigarettes into your pretty ears, and you'd say whatever they wished. You'd implicate others, no matter how strong your ideals seem to you now. Not a soul would stand by you then, Sophie."

"You can't look at things that way, Alex." Sophie was trying hard to be patient. "We must plan on everything going well. I've never seen you lose your self-confidence before."

"I haven't yet. It's simply that we must make every effort to minimize the risk."

They had taken chances before, reckless ones. They agreed to take no unnecessary risks in future. Dropping the name White Rose might help disassociate them from a careless past. Also, there was an artist's studio not far away which belonged to a friend now at the front. It would be a safer place to keep the hectograph than their apart-

167

ment. Aglow with comradeship and conspiracy, Sophie agreed with these provisions eagerly. Over and over she used the word "we," and Hans saw his world overturning as irrevocably as a goldfish bowl.

"If only we hadn't wasted so much time!" she said.

"*Pax! Pax vobiscum!*" exclaimed Hans, raising two fingers in papal benediction. "Think of the Blessed Babe this holy night." But no matter how irreverent his distraction, Sophie would not laugh again. She would not be deflected from her conspiracy. Nor would Alex, who said, "The Christmas elves haven't been entirely idle. They visited Professor Huber's home in Grafelfing. And the good professor has agreed to prepare them a leaflet concerned with a federated Germany after the war."

For a long time Hans had resisted endangering Huber. It was hard enough to build up any resistance to the Nazis. It would be harder and still more important to have a functional plan for Germany when the Third Reich lay in ruins. For this, Hans admitted, they needed the professor's judgment to season their vision, his realism to balance their utopianism.

A few other student-soldiers, like Willi Graf and his friends in the Ruhr, had been sounded out at the Russian front. Most were home now, attending universities in Berlin, Hamburg, and Freiburg. In Stuttgart, Hans and Susanne Hirzel had agreed to distribute leaflets. The original three had become a dozen or more, loosely linked. For a time they had hoped to contact a larger German resistance movement, but, like themselves, it existed only in small, frightened pockets. Certain intellectuals supposedly sat long over their schnapps, planning an ideal state for the future.

Others—in the army high command, it was rumored—plotted the death of Hitler. But these were unverifiable reports, as likely as not spread by Gestapo infiltrators. Hans and his friends were all students. They relied on their own kind, and on few of them. The larger the organization, the greater the chance that one misjudgment could bring them all down.

"What about Christl?" asked Sophie.

Thus far Hans had held his tongue. He always hesitated to put others in hazard, or to compound the risk of exposure, which increased with each new recruit. Christl at least must be safe. "I don't want a family man in this. He's got enough responsibility with two children. Anyway, his wife's nervous enough. She talked herself into thinking she had cancer, and almost convinced her doctor. No, not Christl."

"But Hans, Christl's such a dedicated person," Sophie insisted. "He's exactly the sort we need. Leave the decision up to him." Her low voice was full of confidence as she added, "There were so few of us last summer; so many now."

"When I was small," said Alex, "I went to a circus. I saw the most wonderful sight. A couple of clowns were walking on a tightrope. Then there were more and more of them. I kept wondering how many more clowns before the rope broke."

"And on that optimistic note," said Hans, "may I again suggest a little Christmas cheer? Sophie, bring us some of your biscuits. And something for drinking a toast." When three glasses were filled, Alex proposed, "To us. To good times past, better times to come." They all drank. "Do you

169

remember how we first met, Sophie? In that awful art gallery. You looked so pretty and so disgusted, I had to tell you I also thought Nazi art was frightful."

"I haven't forgotten what I answered. I said, 'I like you, too.' Then I was shocked at myself for saying that to a stranger."

They had shared a coffee afterwards, relishing their contempt for Party aesthetics. Only when they had exchanged names and addresses had they realized their connection through Hans.

"Well, here's to you, Sophie. May your eyes always shine as they're shining now." A cookie in her mouth, she looked at him with a funny, full-lipped smile, the corners of her mouth turned down tight. A wild look of agreeableness strained her chewing features. She swallowed and gave a gasp before addressing him with a remark that changed in midsentence into a coughing laugh.

"Wait . . . I'm trying . . ." She raised her glass. "To the Allies. May they win next year. And to you both, Alex and Hans. To the two finest painters in the world."

"Hear! Hear!" said Alex enthusiastically. "We should paint that on the walls from one end of Ludwigstrasse to the other. Especially the last part."

As though cued by these remarks, there came a knocking at the door. They all rose, listening, waiting for the hand upon the latch. The silence extended itself until it seemed the caller had gone away. Then the rapping came again, not loud but insistent.

"They know we're here," said Alex.

"Maybe it's Christl," said Sophie. "I'll see." She went to the door and flung it open. Feet together, clad in black from head to toe, Franz stood there smiling painfully in

170

greeting, a jack-o-lantern grin that revealed his pale gums.

"Merry Christmas to all of you," he said. "You look surprised. I'm not such a black Nazi that I've given up Christmas. Am I intruding?"

"Not at all, Franz. Come in. Merry Christmas. I believe you know everyone here." Hans's voice rang heartily with forced delight.

"Fräulein Scholl. More lovely than ever." Franz very formally kissed her hand, then sauntered around the room, his head wagging from side to side, his boots sounding solid and sure. "You all became so quiet . . . like little mice. I thought I heard you toasting victory." A chill of terror went through Hans.

Alex ran his tongue around his lips and spat away a little crumb of biscuit. "It's a night to toast everyone," he said, lifting his glass. "To our beloved Führer."

"And a night to slap paint on the walls, yes?"

"Of course, Franz. Imagine 'Joy to the World' plastered all over town. It would do poor dark Munich good."

Franz gave a dry laugh. "Join us," Hans said to him. "Perhaps we might sing a carol."

"I am Saint Nicholas tonight," said Franz. "Your own black Saint Nicholas. Some kirsch, gentlemen. Not easy to get. And a little wurst, fraulein. The real thing, and no ration points required."

Hans opened the kirsch. He put four small glasses on the table and poured. Together with Franz they all raised their glasses solemnly. "To the fatted calves," Franz said enigmatically. Then they sang, one carol after another, and from Franz's black uniform a little darkness seemed to drain.

CHAPTER ELEVEN

● Franz leaned against the cell door. "I wish it were
that Christmas again," he mused. "I should have spoken
to you more firmly then. Believe me, Hans, I'm not tor-
menting you without reason. Even now it may not be too
late. There are other ways out for you."

"I want my life."

"You've already rejected the idea of insanity. Properly,
I think. But there are other ways. You might try to escape.
It would be dangerous and difficult."

"I'm not the sort, Franz. I wouldn't make it."

"Clemency," suggested Franz. "You might ask for
clemency due to your war record, but it's a small chance
with Germany in a black mood. Hitler might commute
the sentence as a gesture, but one can hardly rely on that.
There is only one real hope. You must sign a confession,
Hans. Be deprived of your martyrdom. Admit your
crime. Say you've erred. Make this confession in writing.
Admit developing a deviation; name names of confeder-

ates, but only those who have died at the front. Admit you were shocked when you realized how far they were prepared to go. Such a confession will help the Party by discouraging student demonstrations. For such cooperation, you will probably live."

Hans paced up and down. His body told him to stay alive at any price, but his mind was in turmoil.

"Does it seem cold to you in here?" asked Franz. His arms were pressed close to his sides.

Hans wasn't cold. In fact, he was dripping with perspiration. In an unheated cell in midwinter, his body was drenched with sweat.

"If I recant, would I be freed?"

"No, prison; but alive."

"You mean a natural death from starvation in Dachau."

"No, Hans, you're wrong. They need medical orderlies. You'd receive special consideration in the camp hospital."

"Franz, have you some particular interest in this confession? A promotion?" Hans was thinking of Franz's father, and the consequences of his 'confession' and death.

"Oh, Hans, that hurts. I didn't expect that from you." Franz turned away to hide the emotion in his face. "After I've stuck my neck out for you, time and again."

"I'm sorry, Franz. I didn't mean that. These last few days . . . I'm not quite myself."

"I know. It's been hell for you. But it can get worse, Hans. Or better. Look at it this way. If you worked in a camp, you'd be doing good. You'd be saving lives. That's what you want, isn't it?"

"But I would have to say everything I believe in is morally evil."

"Of course. But if Germany wins, you're that much

better off. If we lose, that's the time to recant. Idealists always thrive after a war."

Hans was tempted. "Does this apply to Sophie as well? she's worked in a hospital, you know."

"Possibly."

"Will you speak to her, Franz? If she . . . speak to me and tell me how she feels."

Franz went immediately, leaving Hans alone. Sophie would not confess to anything, Hans felt sure. Part of him hoped that she would share the guilt of confession. Another part, he knew, would be disappointed, as he had been disappointed in his father. Then, too, it might all be a fraud. He wanted to trust Franz, but even Franz might have been duped. Then he would be signing a confession for nothing. He would not even have the chance of dying with honor. Did he really want to live, no matter how? Disgraced, exiled, imprisoned, any way at all? Surely the last thing one gave up was life.

The pattern of bars cast by the sun on the opposite wall had reddened and compressed itself into the corner when Franz returned. With the door locked again behind him, he slumped down on the other bunk. Hans looked at him. "She refused to confess," he said.

Franz moved his head slowly from side to side. "She insists the Nazis are the criminals, that they should confess. I don't understand you Scholls. Perhaps she didn't believe I came from you, Hans. She said to tell you that it was all right. That you should confess if you wanted to."

"But she wouldn't."

"No, but she's different, Hans. She has all the impenetrability of a Christian martyr. She seems to imagine

God is her accomplice in this business. She's Joan of Arc. Life won't be a success for her until she's burned at the stake."

"If there are saints," said Hans, "Sophie is one."

"Odd that there should be such an equation between martyrs and saints, and . . . oh, forget it."

"Say it, Franz."

"Lunatics. It's all right if you have her beliefs, but I don't think you have. What in hell makes you so set on dying, Hans?"

"Do you suppose the blood that beats in me is any less anxious to keep right on than yours is?"

"Is it heaven, Hans? Do you believe in heaven?"

"You know I don't."

"Then what? Reincarnation? Fame after death? No one will remember you."

"I don't believe in any of those things. That's not the point."

"Just dead and nothing remaining? Forgotten?" Franz dropped his eyes. "Is there nothing I can do?"

"What is there to do? I'm too poor to make a will."

Franz stood up. He seemed to need the wall for support. "All right, Hans. Think it over. You have tonight. There isn't much time left, but it's not too late to change your mind."

So Hans was left with his thoughts. His cellmate returned, looked at him, said nothing, lay down and slept. Outside the wind changed. A thin rain began, and Hans listened for the noises of the muffled city, the clanging of streetcars, the voices of the living. The night was silent except for the rain. It must be very late or very early, then. The ticking of a clock in the corridor created in

176

his mind the unbroken procession of time, like drops from the slowly-leaking sink faucet. One . . . two . . . three . . .

The chances were very good that within twenty-four hours, if he did nothing, he would be dead. Surely enduring death was easier than imagining it. He need only mount the scaffold. Franz had said there was no scaffold at Stadelheim, but Hans pictured one because it gave his mind something to grasp. It was a way of leaving the world behind. But the guillotine! To die as a chicken dies, without the chicken's advantage of ignorance. Yet a chicken cries out, while a man can keep still—sometimes. If, by some incredible accident, the blade failed, they would do it all over again, so the highest hope of a condemned man was that the machinery was in functioning order. As a soldier, he might claim the right to a firing squad. He had considered that, but the thought of all those barrels boring into his eyes brought no comfort.

Some said a life was not wasted if one's death was a triumph. But the Nazis killed and left no trace. Hans remembered once passing the tombs of Crusaders in a cathedral crypt. He remembered the terrible stony repose of those effigies of life, archaic handiwork without humanity. Then, just as he was departing, the appearance of one had stopped him. It was different. Perhaps a stonemason's chisel had slipped, giving the stone mouth a twist, for there was irony in that wry smile, and all at once the army of granite dead was broken. Among them lay a human being. But surely there was little satisfaction in such immortality.

There were other ways. Franz had mentioned escape, but the door was iron and two inches thick, the window

**177**

fixed with interlinking bars. The only sure escape was confession. Confession, humiliation, desertion of Sophie. Hans went to the basin and tried to shut off the leak. The dripping continued, so he put the rag of towel under the faucet. Whether he heard them or not, the drops fell, the dawn would come, and with it the trial. If he confessed his sin, Sophie would forgive him. If he did not, he must take her by the hand and die. But she held fast to God with her other hand. Even after death, she would hold God's hand. She would have her victory. She would escape the despotism of time altogether. For some prisoners, God's face had been known to take form upon the gray prison walls. If only the air would whirl and congeal, he would wrestle with God like Jacob of old. But he had lost his old God, the comforter of his childhood. He had lost him at the Oktoberfest in Munich, and in France, and again in Russia. God had not shown himself in the foxholes or in the craters or in the locked freight cars. God had not whispered to him from the operating tables. So what would God be doing behind the stone walls of Stadelheim Prison?

Though the room was cold, sweat kept pouring out of his body. He went to the small sink, washed himself, and dried off with the gray end of damp toweling. There was the beating of his heart, the slight blue tracery of veins beneath his skin. This was his life, which tomorrow they might spill as swiftly as wine from an uncorked bottle.

If Sophie remained stubborn beyond reason, surely he need not follow her. For the sake of his suffering parents alone, he ought to stay alive. Both of them should, but of all the arguments that marshaled themselves in his mind, one always came first, could not be denied or argued against: the preservation of life itself. Simply to remain alive.

Outside in the night a voice began to sing, a high, sad voice, rising and falling. It reminded Hans of carefree nights in the open air, and he felt a fierce longing for freedom; the most basic, physical kind of freedom. He saw himself get up and make a rush, smashing headlong through the wall, but the real Hans still lay on his back and stared at the wall and tried to recall a green place lost in the mountains. Alex would be there; Alex, for whom life was a marvelous composition of bright colors and fragrances. "Pom, pom, pomity-pom." He thought of Alex tuning his balalaika. He was glad Alex had gotten away. He saw himself there, too, on light feet, never tiring, and for a time the lovely vision managed to keep the contradictions of life and death apart.

Alex had always said life should be led like a last holiday, taking risks for excitement but never becoming entrapped by conviction. "In my country there's only one capital crime: gloom. In my country, a gloomy man loses his head. We don't even walk there as you do." And with surprising agility for one so tall, Alex had stood on his hands, taking a few staggering steps. His left trouser leg had slid down and his upside-down eyes had bulged like those of an alarmed octopus. Finally he had tumbled, and lay still. "O, Lord, I've broken it," he had said, holding his chest. Hans had thought he was referring to a rib, and had rushed to his side, but Alex had made a joke of it. "Not my ribs, you idiot. My pipe." He had gone on all evening with his revels, and it wasn't until days later that Hans had seen the tape around his chest and found out that he had fractured a rib in his fall—in fact, not one rib, but two. That was Alex. This might very likely be his last night in Germany; after that, the ocean. Hans imagined him sailing off in a small ship with the wind of freedom swelling his sail and the jeweled hilt of the Southern Cross rising above the ocean. Yet surely it would be a long and lonesome trail without any ending. Not even Alex could desert them so easily, and he remembered his friends saying, "Do you want to know the sentimental, disgusting truth, Hans? I've been rather haunted by your sister this summer. That low voice of hers, those marvelous, sad eyes." Would there be any place far enough to get away from them?

Well, Alex would take care of Alex. It was Christl he pitied. Christl, who had never liked danger, who had children and a sick wife on his hands. If it had not been for his own terrible negligence in not destroying the handwritten draft, Christl would at least have had Alex's chance of escape. Perhaps a plea of insanity would work for him. Surely his dependent family would be a mitigating circumstance. "If only one of us is to be saved," Hans whispered to the cell walls, "let it be Christl."

Poor Christl. It was weeks now since he had seen him on a depressing January day of mud-ravaged snow, a day full of the news that Stalingrad was dying. Hans had received a letter from Otto that morning. At first the name had not registered, but then he realized it came from his old troop leader, whom he had struck years before and not seen since. The letter had been addressed to Ulm and forwarded from there. It began:

180

Greetings from Stalingrad,

Does it surprise you to hear from an old friend? It surprises me that I am writing this last letter to you. Have no doubt it is the last, and if you wonder why I write, I think it is because, of all the people I have ever known, you are the one back home who might be able to understand what is happening here, and why. So I am writing this once, then never again. Afterward, perhaps, I will haunt your dreams. If my handwriting looks strange, be informed that it is not mine. From frostbite I have lost two fingers on my left hand, and the three middle fingers of my right. It is surprising how clumsy this makes one even when it comes to the simplest tasks. My hands are useless except in one respect. I can shoot. Perhaps I should run a shooting gallery after the war. Will there be shooting galleries? Or even Germany, for that matter? That is no concern of mine. I do not intend to go into explanations that might sound sentimental. We are very near the end. I think within a few days there will not be one of us left here alive. Has the Fuhrer failed us? Once I could not have asked that question, and I don't know the answer now. Some say so. I could not say this to my father. Perhaps I should not say it to you, but it doesn't matter. Do not look to the Sixth Army for an explanation. Look to yourselves. Be on guard so that a greater disaster does not overtake our country. Let the hell on the Volga be a warning to you. My turn is all but over. I have only to manipulate one finger through the motions of firing six shiny bullets. Now it's time to crawl a bit deeper into the ground. Old friend, you may save yourself a reply. I know that will disappoint you, but think of what I have said in two weeks' time. What it will actually be like here, I hope you will never know. Defend your own flag to the death.

Your friend, Otto

Franz's flag. Hans had almost forgotten about it. Strange. He was still puzzling over the contents of Otto's letter and wondering how it had escaped the censors when the phone rang. It was Christl, and the moment Hans heard his voice over the wire he wished he had not picked up the corridor telephone. Christl was despondent. His wife's pregnancy was not going well. She had gained fifteen pounds from worry. He had lost ten for the same reason. He wished the day he was born could be torn from the calendar. The only thing that made life worth living was studying the catechism. He had been visiting a priest regularly and hoped soon to receive absolution. Hans tried to ring off, but Christl begged for a meeting at Lombardi's; just the two of them, for a few minutes. There was evidently something important which couldn't be discussed over a tapped line.

Christl was already there when Hans arrived at the restaurant. Slumped in a chair, he raised his head as Hans drew near. "Don't reproach me, Hans. I haven't been avoiding you. Honestly I haven't. You don't know what these last weeks have been like. I'm so nervous, my teeth keep chattering. I nearly bit through a glass the other day."

"Get hold of yourself, old man. You look as if you're going to pieces."

"Going? Hans, I've gone. You know, I always wanted to do one thing well, really well. Once I won a ping-pong tournament. But this pamphlet business is the first important . . . listen, Hans. I thought . . . now don't reproach me . . . my wife, Herta . . . the new baby . . ." He drew some papers from his pocket. They rattled in his hands.

"Christl, you're doing the right thing, staying out of this. I mean that."

"Just once I thought I could do something important. I can't, Hans."

"You can be a first-class father, Christl. You can give your children a better life."

Christl pushed the handwritten sheets across the table. "I've written something, Hans." It was the draft for a leaflet. Hans quickly concealed it in his pocket.

"We'll make good use of it," he promised. "Christl, have you attended classes at all? You're so pale. Don't mope around at home. That won't do Herta any good."

"She's a sick girl, Hans. She needs help with the other children."

"I'm sorry, Christl. But glooming around won't help her. Try to cheer her up."

"You're right, Hans. And I shouldn't have bothered you. I shouldn't keep you. I can guess how busy you are."

Hans did not argue the point. He wanted to get away. They parted with a clasping of hands that Hans did his best to make fervent.

He had not seen Christl since.

If news from Stalingrad, Otto's letter, and Christl's

despair made for vague and formless fears, they took shape abruptly as Hans walked home alone from Lombardi's. It was drizzling. Late classes were emptying out of the University buildings. Students were scudding home like sailboats under their umbrellas or gathering to talk in doorways. Hans hailed a friend here and there, but he did not stop. There were footfalls behind him as he crossed the street—boots. He walked steadily, turned a corner. The boots followed. He wanted to run, but his mind held his legs in check. In a moment he was overtaken.

"Hans, slow down. I have to speak to you." It was Franz. He put a good deal of intensity into his handshake.

"Which way are you going?" Hans inquired.

"Your way." Drops of water clung to Franz's pale eyelashes.

"I'm on my way home," Hans said.

"Good. I'll come with you."

"You have a great deal of self-confidence these days, Franz. Is there something I can do for you?" Franz did not answer. He walked by Hans's side silently. Not a word passed between them for nearly a quarter of a mile. Then Hans said, "Look here, Franz. Surely it's not merely the pleasure of my company on a day like this."

"It isn't," Franz replied. "But I must make sure we're alone. Hans, we've always been friends. At least, I hope so. I've always admired you, and if I seem like rancid butter, remember I'm on your side of the bread." He laughed lightly. "Hans, have you ever done any hunting?"

"Never."

"Neither have I, but I've been told about it. Do you know the one thing a hunter hates? It's finishing off the

184

quarry. Sometimes a hunter will sit for hours with the beast in his sights, not wanting to destroy the silence. For ever so long the animal may go on cropping the grass, not having the slightest idea. If it only could know without lifting its head . . . if it were given the chance to disappear suddenly . . . perhaps then . . ."

"You have something to say, Franz. Speak frankly, won't you?"

"Well," Franz fingered his chin nervously, "well . . ." Was he gathering strength for a great evasion or a great confession? "I've known you for a long time, Hans. I've measured you. And if I'm mistaken about you, or if you're not the sort of person I imagine, this could mean my life."

"Yes, Franz; go on."

Franz seemed unable to get to the point. "You know, we in the SS are subordinated to the Gestapo. We keep their prisons. If need be, we do their killing. I know the Gestapo. They have no soul, no humanity. They never say, "You were a good sport, old man. Go home and don't do it again." They are more thorough, Hans, than a forest fire. They miss nothing; a smudged fingerprint, a single hair, a shred of silk. Even a chance remark dropped casually without malice. There is no hunter in this world, Hans, so certain of its quarry."

"You paint a very clear picture, Franz. What's the point?"

"You are the quarry I was speaking of. You're in their sights even now; you, and certain others." This stopped Hans in his tracks. It stopped his brain and his heart. "But Hans, that isn't necessarily fatal. The hunter waits, reluctant. One suspicious move on the animal's part, and he will pull the trigger. Don't make that move, Hans. Vanish quickly. You have no choice. That's all, Hans. I've taken a great risk in warning you. I can't do anything more. It's up to you now."

Hans arrived home shaken. His first thought was of an escape kit: climbing shoes, a knapsack full of dried meat and fruit to last a week. He would go the way they had taken Herr Bittner, and he would take Sophie and Alex with him. It was all set in his mind, and when Sophie returned from class, he told her everything.

"I'm not surprised," she said. "Isn't everyone in Germany under surveillance?"

"We're not playing Alex's game anymore. We must think things out, Sophie."

"Think what out?"

"You are so unbelievably pig-headed!" he told her. "Our lives are at stake, Sophie. Our lives! We must get out of Germany. What do you suggest we do, put a sign on the door? "This is the home of two poor students who have given the last ten years of their lives to National Socialism. There is nothing of interest or value here. Salute your Führer. Gestapo and SS please pass by." Is that the sort of precaution you approve of?"

"If you like, I'll make a sign for you," she said with weary patience. "Hans, I know you're worried for all of us. It's just that I know, without a doubt, that what I'm doing is right. I can't see beyond that."

That was what worried him; her complete disregard for security. She never seemed to realize that even the classrooms were full of informers. Some were paid Gestapo agents, others thought of themselves as patriotic Germans who, with a heavy sense of duty, would report subversive remarks. Sophie was just as careless around the apartment with written evidence. "This stuff can't go out with the trash," he would tell her. Those notes that had served their purpose he burned in a metal wastebasket, mixed the ashes with water, and put them down the sink. Still-valuable material he kept in a false bottom he had fashioned for the waste basket. He had meant to put Christl's draft there, but in the heat of his argument with Sophie he forgot all about it.

Hans took a few angry turns around the apartment. He burned an undecipherable sheet covered with Sophie's writing, only to be coldly informed that it was the first draft of a philosophy paper. "Listen," he whispered furiously, "you and I are going for a walk this evening. If we're not followed, we can thrash this out once and for all. Can't you get it through your thick head that even the walls of this apartment may be wired?"

It was cold that night. The city had been recently bombed, so that they could not tell from the crunching underfoot whether they had stepped through frozen puddles or on broken window glass. They crossed the Ludwigstrasse. A triumphal arch barred the far end, rearing up like a tombstone in the moonlight. Here Hitler had paraded with the ghosts of Caesars. Flattened against the wall on the far side was a bombed-out automobile. The wall above the car bore the legend, "God is Love."

In silence they entered the English Garden.

"Alex and I always talk of coming here to sketch. We never do," said Sophie. "He ought to be with us tonight. I promised Mother I would bring him home to meet her this spring. She'd be scared to death if she knew what we were doing."

"She's more intuitive than you think," Hans assured her. "She knows. I think she knows more than Father does. That's just one more reason—"

"Look, Hans. The river looks so mysterious in the moonlight."

"Sophie, I've done one practical thing. I've been putting together a kit in case . . . well, in case we want to get away. It's sort of an escape kit, you know. Bandages, chocolate . . . yes, chocolate, believe it or not. I even got hold of some cocaine and dried blood from the hospital lab. It throws off bloodhounds; did you know that?" He wanted her to comment, but she didn't. "You know, Sophie, we could escape anytime to Switzerland. This could be our last night in Germany." She did not reply, but he fancied he knew her mind. "I don't mean forever. We'd come back when we could be more useful. Even if we stayed away until the war ended, we've tried harder than anyone else. In Munich, who else has painted slogans? No one. No one else has put out a leaflet. We've done more than our share. They say Zurich's a nice city. We could spend all day deciding whether to buy a green or a blue fountain pen. We could sit in the library reading, a passage here and a passage there. They have good medical schools in Switzerland, Sophie. Or we could just enjoy nature, away from all this. I'd shear sheep and you'd make butter. We'd have long, happy, quiet lives. I'd go fishing—"

"We couldn't leave Alex behind."

"Of course Alex would come," Hans said. "You'd get married and he'd make cuckoo clocks. You'd have a big family. I wouldn't mind marrying some pretty Swiss girl myself and having a child. A child says something about a person; that you were here. Sophie, are you listening?" She gave an almost imperceptible nod. "No matter what I say lately, you're always so far away."

"I'm not," she protested.

"Yes," he replied. "You always are. You're becoming like Christl."

"I'm not. If it seems that way, it's because you're dreaming, Hans. I know it and you do, too."

"If Alex and I went to Switzerland, you couldn't go on without us."

"But I would, Hans. I'm like a bulldog. I hang on."

Hans caught her arm. "Be quiet! I think we're being followed," he whispered. With the double awareness he had developed in the last weeks, he heard a cry far off. But it was only a sound that the darkness made; the Isar passing and changing tone. If they were followed among the trees, they would not know it. The shimmering moon gave ghostly outline to a naked human figure. The sight drew from both of them an involuntary gasp. Then just as automatically they laughed to the verge of hysteria. "Oh, my side," Hans managed. "Sophie, we're falling apart; we really are." Hand in hand they circled once around the statue, then took the bridge that led away from Schwabing and their apartment. They found themselves flanked by a high iron picket fence behind which trees swayed gently, their bare branches washed by metallic moonlight.

"I think there's a cemetery in there." Hans's remark was verified by a sign on the gate. As he read it, he felt minute pinpricks creep over his face like invisible frost.

189

"It's Perlacher cemetery," he said. A star that had been hanging in a tree branch hid itself behind the limb. "Where they take political prisoners and put them down in unmarked graves."

"So many have been killed," Sophie said, "it seems almost indecent to remain alive." For Hans such speculations had very little to do with the observable facts of life. If one swallowed death, one did not spit it out. Heaven was too high for him. Earth was good enough. Death could only thrust him underground, not nearer to God. "Don't be afraid, Hans. As long as we stick together, what can happen?"

"Pretend you're standing on my grave," he said.

"You only think you're afraid, Hans." This was not criticism. There was wonder, even worship, in the way she looked at him. "The rest of us have only followed your lead all along."

"If we're caught, we'll probably end up here, forgotten. Even if the Nazis let us live, it would mean Ravensbruck for you and Dachau for me, with a red chevron on our shoulders and not much hope of coming out alive."

Weary of walking, they boarded a streetcar bound for Schwabing. They had amused, frightened, annoyed, and finally exhausted each other without resolving anything. The streetcar was empty and smelled of sweat. Then two little girls climbed aboard. "Lord knows why they're loose at this hour," Hans said. Sophie thought they came from a party. One carried a doll. She turned its head around on its body to look at Hans. The two children sang a birthday song in fragile voices. Then they began a popular ballad with altered lines.

190

"Everything passes over,
Everything passes by;
Even Adolph Hitler,
Even his Party."


Hans could hardly believe his ears. "They don't know what they're singing. They can't know."

"No, said Sophie, "but someone taught them. That's what's important."

The streetcar had recrossed the Isar by the time the children got out. A breeze from the river tossed back their young laughter as they linked arms and pranced away like carousel ponies.

The door closed, the tram rolled on.

"Hans, do you remember when I worked with the retarded children? You know what happened to them. They never had a chance. None of these poor children do, if there aren't a few people in Germany with a conscience. You know that's true. Say we'll try one more time." Her interminable "we," thought Hans, as though he were some sly Siamese twin who might detach himself and vanish.

"One leaflet, Sophie. One quick distribution, and then you agree to escape?"

"That's a promise," she said, but the second part of the bargain was small in her mind. "Hans, I believe a leaflet scattered at the right time could start an uprising among the students. It could spread all over the city. There's no telling where it would stop."

"But it's no good simply tearing things down, Sophie. That's easy, compared to rebuilding."

"But tearing down comes first. In Germany it has to come first."

Were they trying to rework reality, or was reality reworking them? Hans was not sure, but somehow their conversation on the slow streetcar, feeling its blind way through the blackout, held all the aspects of a dialogue with fate. Hans had talked and listened, but Sophie had won, and always in her victory there was an unselfish part of himself. For a while he would have renewed faith—if not in God, then in Sophie and her conscience, which was a mirror of his own. But they needed more than faith. They needed a miracle. If they succeeded, he told himself, he would never again question the ways of God. If they failed, they could try for Switzerland and the good, Godless life.

The blacked-out streetcar groped through a right turn into Ludwigstrasse just as a siren sounded in the distance. It rolled on until a nearer warning brought it to a standstill in the center of the wide avenue. Sophie and Hans got out and began to walk.

"I'll have to go down to the hospital when it's over," Hans said gloomily. It had become a regular assignment, trying to reassemble the poor jigsawed victims, trying to breathe life into their ruined bodies.

Fortunately they weren't far from their flat. They linked arms, each feeling almost frightened by the intensity of comradeship the other's touch induced. No bombs could touch them. Sophie was as convinced of that as she was convinced of their eventual success. For the moment, Hans shared her confidence. A dreadful inadvertency governed their actions; nor did they make any effort—and here Hans realized he had lost himself completely—to avert whatever fate might be in store for them. Let the bombs fall. They were children awaiting a spring shower.

192

The old spectator raids were over, and a warden, striking his shelter gong, accosted them angrily. He made them take cover in one of the teardrop shelters of reinforced concrete that had been built in high-priority target areas. "Watch the steps!" he shouted after them. The steps were icy. Hans gripped Sophie's arm to keep her from slipping as above them the sky began to crack and boom.

# CHAPTER TWELVE

● The solitary bulb burned overhead. The cell was gray, the window black. Hans's fellow prisoner lay curled on his wooden shelf, but Hans did not want to sleep. He meant to sift those last days for something of indestructible value. If Franz knew what he was talking about, they would be tried in the morning, sentenced in the afternoon, and, if nothing was done to alter the circumstances, executed or incarcerated before dark.

The days of the last leaflet had begun almost like a spree. Alex had turned up with two buckets of prewar paint. "Saul's haunting me tonight," he had told Hans. "I can't sleep." Together they had stolen up and down the blacked-out Ludwigstrasse, painting surprises for Sophie.

"About seventy of them," Alex told her gaily.

"Don't be so secretive," she demanded. "Tell me what you wrote."

"Seventy times in big red letters: 'I love you, Sophie Scholl.'"

But the signs the next morning's light revealed on the parade street had actually read, "Hitler the Mass Murderer" and "The Jews Will Be Revenged." "Freedom" was painted over the University entrance. Two washerwomen had been trying to rub it out when Sophie arrived for class. "Let the people read it," she had admonished them, but they were forced laborers fresh from Russia and could not understand.

Sign painting was only a dangerous prank, Sophie let them know. They ought to be preparing the last leaflet so that it would be ready when the moment of provocation arrived. She was right. Hans knew that, but as she lacked insistence, he lacked initiative. It was as if the rarefied air of conspiracy and hazard had exhausted them both. Simply forming the resolve had taken all their strength. They needed time to breathe before pressing their decision home. Besides, Hans argued, what was the use of a pamphlet that had no connection with public sentiment? All they could do was wait for an incident on which to base it, so they were unprepared when the event occurred.

The moment they had anticipated with mingled hope and dread came suddenly. The University body was summoned to the German Museum to hear a speech by Gauleiter Giessler of Bavaria on how scholars should conduct themselves in wartime. For Giessler, mediocrity was a goal and vulgarity a virtue. His address to the male students brought a derisive shuffling of feet. When he turned to the girls, he said, "You have healthy bodies. You must bear children. There is no reason why every female student should not, for each of her years at the University, present an annual testimonial in the form of a son."

196

Though the drumming of feet had grown louder, the Gauleiter continued, leeringly, "I realize that some co-operation is necessary, and if any of you females lack sufficient allure to find a mate, I can assign you one of my adjutants, whose antecedents I can vouch for."

Here he paused to give his audience a chance to appraise the swastika-wearing attendants behind him. There was a breathless silence throughout the hall.

The reaction began almost inaudibly. A few feet began to drum the floor again, then more and more, until the hall filled with rumbling protest. The adjutants of whom the Gauleiter had spoken moved into the audience to restore attention. One student was dragged to his feet, fought back, and was felled. With this, the storm broke. Many of the Nazis were beaten senseless, others were thrown down the stairs. Gauleiter Giessler vanished from the hall as students erupted into the street. All that day the University was in ferment. Classes were suspended, and armored cars toured the main avenues of Munich.

When Hans and Sophie met that evening, she said, "Any man who has the conceit to stand up there and refer to us as 'females . . .' There isn't a girl in Munich who wouldn't string him to a lamppost just for using that word. We must do it now, Hans."

"Lynch the dear Gauleiter? Why not?"

"No, I mean the last leaflet."

"I know," he agreed. "As soon as possible." Hans realized, as Sophie did not, that before a leaflet could be written, printed, and distributed, the mood of the students could fade. But he felt driven to conclude their last venture one way or another, so he said, "I'll get in touch with Alex tonight."

"And Professor Huber. He's already prepared a draft."

Yet with Alex and Hans on ambulance call during that night's air raid, the four could not assemble until the following night. Already a day had been squandered, but Hans found himself incapable of moving rapidly, like a priest involved in a sacred ritual.

Alex was the first to arrive. He held a smoking pipe in one hand and Sophie with the other. "I wouldn't be here if you weren't so lovely. I fell asleep in the lecture hall this morning. If these raids keep up, it's the only sleep I'll get."

"Of course you'd be here, Alex." She appeared gay and full of confidence.

"Have a look outside, Hans, while I give your sister a kiss," Alex said. "I saw a man loitering out there in the street."

Peering from behind the blackout curtain, Hans saw nothing suspicious. "Here comes Professor Huber," he said with relief. It was never easy to put aside the thought of surveillance.

They placed chairs around the small table that had borne so many secret papers before, but when he arrived, Professor Huber refused to sit. Some time before, Hans had shown him one of the leaflets.

The Professor had read it through silently. "This," he had said slowly, "is remarkable. Very. It's dangerous, Hans, but it's wonderful, too. You did this."

"I didn't say that."

The Professor had placed his hands on Hans's shoulders. "But you did. I know your style, Hans; don't forget. I'm very proud that you should show me. When the time comes, you shall have my help."

Now the time had come, and the Professor was too

nervous to sit. He paced up and down. The immensity of Germany's defeat at Stalingrad had been too much for him. At first he had been unable to believe it. Then he had sat up all night preparing a manifesto, a call to arms against the Nazi party.

Alex was the first to examine the manifesto. "This is good," he said.

As Hans listened to Alex reading Huber's paper aloud, he agreed. It had quality. There would be no need for any other draft. Christl's, now forgotten, still lay in his pocket.

Sophie exclaimed, "It's wonderful. It's just the thing, if we can add a direct appeal to the students." She wanted a reference to the Gauleiter's speech. Hans backed her up, and Professor Huber agreed to the addition.

"And what about this in here," suggested Alex. " 'The eyes of even the dullest German have been opened by the fearful bloodbath perpetrated against the Jews.' " He read from a bit of scrap paper.

"It's not simply the Jews," Hans said. "It's against all of Europe, the whole world." There was no real argument until Hans drew a line through one of Huber's sentences: "Stand by our glorious army." This became a bone of contention, and they worried it like a pack of bulldogs. If there was any noble tradition in Germany free of Nazi contamination, any structure around which a new Germany could be built, it was the army, argued Professor Huber. But as far as Hans could see, if the Nazis were to fall, the army, too, must go down. There must be an end to all of Germany's power. Professor Huber's pacing became more furious, and his face grew red from his suppressed anger, but Hans was adamant. To endorse the army was to endorse killing. He couldn't do that.

Alex listened to the argument until his pipe went

199

out. Then he gave a great sigh like a burst pipe. "I read in the paper the other day that the implacable resistance of our troops surrounded at Stalingrad was a shining beacon of inspiration to the German people. I can just see a soldier on that field of corpses saying to another, 'There's a funny smell here.' 'Of what?' asks the second soldier. The first soldier replies, 'Of beacons.' "

"I didn't come out on a freezing night to listen to bad jokes," said the Professor. "My God, you children! I worry about my blood pressure. I ought to worry about my sanity. You want to tear the world apart, with no thought of how to put it together again."

"Professor Huber, that isn't so. That's why you're here. Come, please sit down. We'll talk sensibly. No more jokes, Alex." Hans's voice was free of challenge.

"Thank you, no." Perhaps Huber had mistaken Hans's tone. "I'm leaving for Kempten in the morning, in any case. The manuscript is in your hands. As for myself, I shall follow the wise example of Pontius Pilate and say, 'What I have written, I have written.' "

Sophie helped him on with his overcoat. Hans and Alex each gave a little bow of respect as he went out the door.

"And now it's up to the three of us," said Hans. He was relieved. "At least that's one less life we'll be risking."

"All right," said Alex. "We'll print as many copies as we can tomorrow. Right?" Hans nodded affirmation. "That night we'll scatter them around the campus. Then take off for Switzerland."

"There's only one thing," Sophie interrupted. "We won't do it at night. It has to be just before class."

200

"In broad daylight? You can't be serious," said Alex. "We've always worked in the dark before."

"Sophie and I talked about that," Hans said. "You know the classrooms are kept locked until the students begin to arrive in the morning. If we distribute the leaflets the night before, the janitors will sweep them up before any students get there. Besides, if our example isn't bold, how will others find courage to follow? I know what you'll say, but I agree with Sophie."

"But, my God, Hans. That's absolute suicide!"

"Most of the students will stand with us," Sophie urged. "I know it." Her conviction suggested foreknowledge of a settled future.

"They may drum their pencils on their desks. They may even break a little glass and mill around the streets. But that will be all," Alex insisted.

"If nothing happens, we'll clear out fast. You know the arrangements," Hans added. "Alex, I thought you had a taste for this sort of thing."

"Well, I like the feeling of running along the edge of a cliff, if that's what you mean. It's exhilarating while it lasts, and there's always a chance one won't fall. But you people make me feel like Daniel in the wrong den. The only chance for this plan of yours is a miracle, and miracles don't happen nowadays."

"Once I would have agreed with you," said Hans. "Now I'm not sure. Are you with us, or against us, Alex?"

"In theory, I'm with you one hundred percent. But Siegfried's funeral music is running through my head today. Have you ever tried telling a dead man he died a brave death? There's nothing wrong with some contempt for death, but you people . . . This is contempt for life.

You're like Saul. You want to be martyrs. You do! Maybe I'm too healthy for that. Think of all the fanatics who've been crucified. Not fanatics, damn it . . . idiots! All trying to be like Christ."

"And if there had been no Christ?" Sophie whispered. "We would have to do this alone." She was right, thought Hans. If their motives had been fame or glory, he would not go on. But if in some small way they could contribute to the saving of Germany, as ten just men might once have saved Sodom, that was enough. Even if they were forgotten, it was the deed that mattered, not the credit. "Alex," Sophie cried, "please stop playing. I'm frightened."

"Of what, Sophie?"

"Of your glib evasions. For God's sake, Alex, what do you intend?" It was almost a scream.

"I love you." Alex spoke the three words quite hopelessly, as he might have said, "I have cancer." Sophie seemed completely to misinterpret his tone.

"Oh, Alex!" She turned in exasperation to Hans. "Maybe he'll talk seriously to you."

"He is serious, Sophie. He would marry you and keep you safe. I wish you'd take her and drag her out of here, Alex. I would rather be alone in this."

"I'm not a caveman," said Alex. "But the rest of what Hans says is true."

"Oh, Alex." Sophie took his face in her hands and examined it with care and sadness. "What a lovely compliment. I am so fond of you, Alex. But you can't endanger your life on my account. It should have nothing to do with me."

"If you'd only reconsider, Sophie. We can do this at night, as we have before."

She shook her head. "What we've done before has accomplished nothing."

"This way you'll only accomplish your death. Surely it's better to stay alive. There'll be a need for decent Germans after the war. Sophie, please listen to me. Do you think anyone else will follow you where I'm afraid to go?"

"I won't look back to see if anyone is following," she said.

"I'll marry you today. I'll desert the army, become an exile in Switzerland. Anything, Sophie, except commit suicide. Hans, I've told you before—that's where I draw the line."

"I know it," Hans said. "I understand how you feel."

"Sophie, do you despise me for this?"

"Of course I don't, Alex." She seemed stunned and very close to despair. "I love you. I always shall."

"Then come. Now."

"I can't, Alex. There's a great hand pushing me."

Hans felt that hand, too. It was inside him.

"Then I'll wait for you both outside the University." Alex made one last attempt, but the wounded look in Sophie's eyes stopped him. "You're sure? . . . Then I'll check your gear near the station. You'll promise to come then?"

"Yes, when it's done," Sophie said. "Don't worry, Alex. We'll be all right." He took a step toward her, but she stopped him with her words. "There's really no need to worry about me, Alex. Thank you, anyway." For some

203

time they stood there, but there was nothing more to say.

Finally Hans accompanied his friend into the corridor. He gave him a comradely punch. "See you in a couple of days, old man. May you live to be a hundred. If you die, laughter will die with you." Alex looked as though it had died already as he stepped into the dark hallway. Hans held the door open to give him light and listened to his footsteps on the stairs. Then he closed the door.

"Now it's just the two of us," he said to Sophie.

"It always has been," she replied.

# CHAPTER THIRTEEN

● "Fellow Students," began the last leaflet.

It went on to recite the fate of Stalingrad, placing the blame on Hitler and the Nazi party. It cited the Gauleiter's speech and the resistance to it as a first step toward the reconquest of individual rights. It ended, "The dead of Stalingrad abjure you, 'Awake, my people. The beacons are aflame!' Our nation, inspired by a new outburst of faith in Freedom and Honor, is on the move against the enslavement of Europe by National Socialism."

They had planned to do the printing in one night, but an air raid called Hans to the hospital, and they had to return again to the nearby artist's studio where the small copy machine was kept hidden under half-finished canvases. Studies were forgotten. Hans cut the larger lectures, but attended the medical seminars and laboratories in order to avoid suspicion. In the unheated studio, they wore gloves, which did away with fingerprints. Candles were their only source of light. Long before morning they were close to exhaustion. "Sophie," Hans said once, "perhaps we ought to stop. I feel watched." But even that mattered little now, and they toiled on in a kind of dream, without present, past, or future. This last leaflet filled their world. There seemed no will left in Hans to alter their course, no thoughts to weigh their prospects; only the reflexive strength to make copy after copy, to distribute them when the time came, and then, if possible, to survive.

Sometimes they were irritable and spoke sharply.

"You look tired, Hans. Your eyes are red."

"You ought to see them from my side."

"Then for heaven's sake, lie down. Rest."

"That's the last thing I'll do. But I could manage without your nagging." He closed his lips firmly between every phrase. "I am not nervous. I am not thirsty. I simply want to get on with this."

Mostly, during those last nights, they were fond, bound together by many ties. Then Hans would look at his sister toiling in the drafty room, at the arch of her neck as she bent her head over the hectograph machine, the soft brown hair that she would impatiently brush out of her eyes, and he felt as if they had endured together since the beginning of the world. They were so different, yet so much alike, that studying her face was like studying his own.

On Wednesday, the seventeenth day of February, the job was done. A heavy pile of leaflets lay between them. Two people could carry no more.

"It frightens me to look at all those . . . death sentences," said Hans.

"In the morning everything will be all right. You'll

206

see." Her adroitness at self-deception was terrifying. "To-morrow will be wonderful." As though by instinct, they put out their hands to each other. Their cold fingers squeezed hard, and on their faces was exaltation mixed with fear. "Think of it, Hans. Our whole lives may have been designed for tomorrow."

Hans could not help crying. The slowly-oozing tears were born of fatigue and his sister's mystic faith. "For tomorrow," he repeated, and momentarily he believed, along with Sophie, that they had been given a sign, that they would survive whatever lay ahead of them if some-how they clung to each other.

"Let's go home," he told her. "You'll need some sleep for the morning." He doubted that he would ever sleep again. Very few hours of darkness remained.

At dawn, Hans felt Sophie's presence by his bed. She was looking at him skeptically. "You didn't sleep, did you? I could hear you hardly breathing all night."

"You could hear me hardly breathing?" He almost laughed.

"You know what I mean. I'm nervous, too. My hands are shaking horribly." She held them tightly clasped at her waist.

"That's nothing. I've a tic in my left eyelid. Look."

"Hans, I dreamed we were arrested by the Gestapo."

In Sophie's voice he heard the tone of augury. "No one believes in dreams," he said.

Everything was ready. Hans had purchased railroad tickets two days before. Their hiking kits were packed and already in Alex's possession. Two large briefcases were stuffed with leaflets. Picking them up, they went swiftly down the stairs and into the street.

"What a lovely morning," said Sophie. "I can smell spring in the air."

"A false spring. There's still five weeks of winter."

They neither dallied nor hurried, though as they went, their pace accelerated. Sophie appeared visibly to grow younger, more assured, with each stride. Hans grinned at her; she grinned back. The skin felt tight over his cheekbones and his mouth was dry. Suddenly he remembered. "My God, Sophie! We didn't burn the stuff in the bottom of the wastebasket." But there were only a few moments between the unlocking of the classrooms and the arrival of the students and instructors. To return would mean another day's delay. Hans could not steel himself to this again. They would have to return to the apartment afterward and destroy the evidence.

Like two bombs set to explode but for the moment ticking on like ordinary clocks, they turned into Leopoldstrasse. Hans felt as though he had left everything behind. The need to write, to think, to take nourishment—all such needs had evaporated. The dice had rolled. He would not pick them up again. If God, against all likelihood, would bring them success, Hans promised never to doubt His existence again.

They reached the first University buildings. Their walls barred the sun and brought a chill to the air. The great entry hall of the University was colder still.

"Now into thy hands, O Lord Jesus, I commit my spirit." He could barely hear Sophie's whisper as they started up the stairs.

Their intention had been to shower the empty lecture halls with leaflets, but for some reason the custodian had not unlocked them at the usual time. Hans tried one knob after another. All were locked. But they could no more pause and bide their time for a more opportune moment than stones flung from a catapult. Their taut nerves would support no further delay.

Their time was now. Already the first students were clustering before the great bulletin boards in the main hall. The long corridors remained to them, where cleaning women were at work. Hans felt a pounding inside him; not in his chest, but lower, almost in his belly.

"Yes, Sophie," he whispered, opening his case. She took a great handful and headed down one corridor, dropping leaflets as she went.

"Don't clean them up," she called to the scrubwomen. "They're meant to be read." Hans followed another corridor, moving more and more quickly, scattering leaflets like seed. Down one corridor and then the next, always more quickly, like a fox that nears its earth. He could hear a clock from inside one of the halls, and managed to shove a handful of leaflets under the door. The place was full of tickings, like crickets in September grass.

Hans headed back toward the balcony of the entrance hall. He passed two cleaning women who stood together reading the manifesto. They looked at him, their faces noncommittal. Sophie had reached the balcony ahead of him. Both of them still had many leaflets, and they emptied handfuls from the balcony into the entrance hall. Like errant autumn leaves they fell, drifting, tumbling, settling on the floor. The last of Professor Huber's manifesto they carried to the top floor. Hans opened a window above the University's courtyard. Students were already there when Sophie let all the remaining pamphlets fly.

They streamed from her hands as the wind carried them out and down.

"That finishes it," said Hans.

"No, that begins it." She stood with her head turned a little sideways, as if presenting her ear to the window. What was she listening for?

"Sophie, hurry! We've got to hurry!"

Had a shutter across the courtyard moved? The corridor behind them was empty, but Hans was aware of something there, too. No footfall, but an amorphous sense of intrusion.

"There's someone waiting around the corner," he whispered.

They ran swiftly in the other direction, but when they came to the exit door, it was locked.

"This is never locked!" Hans rattled the knob as a cold sediment of blood carried terror to his legs and feet. "We're locked in!" He leaned on the door, then crashed against it with his shoulder. It was heavy oak, built for the ages. They were trapped.

Instinctively they reached out to one another. Hand in hand they walked back slowly, two students early for class, as a beefy figure moved toward them. Hans attempted a bored monologue on the ethics of Nietzsche. Schmid, a University porter, his red face blazing with inquiry, intercepted them. "Are these yours?" he asked incredulously, holding out some leaflets.

"We're students here. I don't know what you're talking about." Hans pulled Sophie along.

"You!" shouted the porter, shoving the papers very close to Hans's face. "You wait! These are yours!"

Hans passed him, but the porter caught hold of his

sleeve. "What's the meaning of this?" Hans tried to sound indignant, but his voice betrayed him. "Take your hands off me. I'll be late for class." He shook himself free of the porter's grasp.

"All the doors are locked," said the man. "You'll do better to come along."

for yourself."

Still hand in hand, they followed the porter.

"Very well," said Hans. "But you're making trouble

"Hans," Sophie whispered, "I dragged you into this."

"Nonsense," he replied softly. They had set themselves a task. Given the circumstances, they could have done no more. Now it was up to the students.

The porter led them to the office of the Secretary, Albert Scheithammer, who spoke to them in a harsh, unfriendly tone, as if he did not enjoy what he must do. Sophie pressed close to Hans. The grip of her fingers on his was tight as a trap, but she stood up straight. He wanted to be a tower of strength for her, but where she drew courage from faith, he had only desperation.

"What is it you intend to do, Herr Scheithammer?" he asked the Secretary. He was astonished at the evenness of his voice.

"Nothing at all. It's not up to me. I'm afraid this is a Gestapo matter."

"Would it be possible for me to talk to you before you call them?"

"It's out of my hands, I regret to say. Do you wish to be seated?" He indicated a bench along the wall.

"May I talk to my sister alone, then?"

"I'm sorry. The Gestapo have already been notified." Boots tramped down the hall. "I'm afraid they're here."

The Secretary stood up as the three Gestapo men entered. There was no ceremony, no interrogation, no delay. One of the men took Sophie by the arm. The other pair stood on either side of Hans, their arms crooked around his in a practiced and quite irresistible grip. He walked between them, their bodies forming an interlocked trinity as rigid as if carved from one block of wood.

It was useless to struggle. Outside the building was their only hope. If the manifesto had aroused the students sufficiently, they might break away into the unruly crowd. But there was no crowd. A few students backed away. They stood with lowered eyes studying the paving stones. Hans looked from face to face, but he saw no succor there.

Some of the students held copies of the pamphlet, as self-conscious as children caught in the jam jar. One of the Gestapo men brought his fist down on a hand holding a leaflet. It fell. Other leaflets were dropped voluntarily.

"Alex! Alex!"

Brought to attention by his sister's voice, Hans recognized his friend among the students.

Alex was dressed for hiking and pale as a corpse. He took a stumbling step toward them, then stopped as the agent who held Sophie by the arm loosened the flap of his holster.

"You, there! Do you know this girl?"

"She studies at the University," replied Alex. The other students had moved away from him. Alex was alone. He could not save them now. He could only throw his own life away.

"Do you know her?"

"Yes, I do."

The agent addressed himself to Sophie. "Is this fellow a friend of yours?"

212

With her lips pressed tightly together, Sophie shook her head slowly. She made no other sign.

They were led to the Gestapo car that waited by the curb. The students stared after them as a red sun rose over the rooftops of the wintry city. The students were few. They could not hope for help, and no help came.

CHAPTER FOURTEEN

● Hans lay still, trying not to breathe, as if this might hold time back. He wasn't exactly cold, but he couldn't feel his arms or his shoulders. He had the impression that something was missing and looked around for his coat, only then remembering that they had taken it from him. Before morning he would freeze solid. His nose was growing into his skull, turning to ice or stone. By morning he would be too hard to move to Dachau, too hard for the guillotine at Stadelheim.

He imagined Sophie sleeping peacefully, even though she hated the cold. Perhaps they had given her a blanket. It would take more than a blanket to warm him; more than a bottle of schnapps. He needed a private faith to steady him. They were going to try to destroy him and what he had attempted to do. Hans could not delude himself into thinking that others would carry on. The torch of the White Rose was extinguished. No matter! What he had done was right, however futile, however much he had bungled or mishandled the details. To have acted otherwise would have been to share forever the guilt of a guilty land. Of this Hans was sure, and it was the only certainty to which he could hold fast. They might annihilate his body, but nothing could touch or tarnish him now except his own cowardice.

The feel and the smell of dawn came long before the outer light. Hans heard men in the courtyard. Were they going to execute him in the dark, without a trial? No matter; he had found the strength that comes with complete hopelessness. Slowly the window bars blended with the graying sky. The night was sinking like dark sediment in old wine bottles, leaving the glass clear. He held his breath and strained his hearing to extract significance from every sound. His whole head was an organ of hearing, his whole body one beating heart. Somewhere guards stamped their feet in the cold. His cellmate stirred in sleep.

They would be coming soon. For the last time Hans bathed himself in the sink, while his mind rehearsed the final act. He heard the last clang of the blade. His own red sob rang silently in his ears. Eyes closed, he held fast to the sink with both hands, but this time he had reached the end. He was as ready as he would ever be.

Presently his cellmate awakened and coughed repeatedly. He spat into a filthy handkerchief. "Good morning," he said, smiling, as though the night together, in which they had not exchanged a word, had created a bond between them.

There were sounds from the corridor. Once or twice something drew from the lock exactly the squeak it made when being opened. Hans sat like a stone on his bed, eyes on the latch. A quick footfall clipped down the corridor like a rain of nails. They were coming! A din of voices mounted in the corridor, and though he had spent the night preparing for this moment, Hans could not master his breathing, nor the beating of his heart. "Be quiet. It's nothing," he told his wildly racing heart as one might address a child during a disaster. Raising himself slightly, he listened. Then the latch turned, and the door opened.

Franz entered. Hans marveled at him. He had the motions of a living person. He shivered in the cold cell as the living are expected to shiver, but he spoke in a series of nervous hesitations, starts and stops, like an uncertain telegrapher. "Hans ? Hans, have you . . . have you thought it over? Have you . . . anything to say to me?"

"I haven't anything to say to anyone." The words might have come from a ventriloquist's dummy, so separate were they from his body, which he seemed able to observe as a thing apart. He was even able to force a smile onto his lips.

"Are you hungry, Hans?"

Desire was dead in him, even for food and drink.

"I know how it is, Hans. It doesn't seem real now, but it will, I promise you, when it's too late. Sign this paper, Hans. It's a confession. It will save you."

"I can't."

"What are you asking of me, Hans? I've tried everything, short of breaking you out of jail."

"I'm not asking anything. You've been a good friend, Franz."

"I'd even try that if I thought you'd cooperate."

Hans was scarcely listening. The sun had just touched the bars above his head with a pearly glow. "Franz, do you know what happens when a country is burned and bombed and its people are all killed in the night, and all is lost, and the guilty and the innocent are dead together? Do you know what happens then, Franz?"

"Hans, what the hell are you talking about?"

"Look at the window, Franz. It's the dawn."

"You're crazy. You'll be executed and buried. You can't—"

"I can, Franz. That's the remarkable thing. I can!"

Franz's face looked shrunken. "I will see you later, Hans. At Stadelheim." Abruptly, he turned and left the cell.

Before the guards arrived, Hans shook hands with his cellmate. "Let's say good-bye while we're still alone," he said. Then he took a pencil. His right hand was shaking, so he held his wrist with the other to steady it. On the wall he wrote: *Allen Gewalten zum Trotz sich heralten*— "In spite of all force maintain thyself." It helped to see it there.

At the same time, though he did not know it then, Sophie was writing on the charge sheet one word: "Freedom."

When they came for him, his legs felt like stilts, but he managed to walk between the guards without stumbling. After four days in confinement, the world was as bright as glass. Here was life, in which he had tried to relinquish all interest. The sun, as it struck his eyes, was blinding.

The Palace of Justice in Munich was a vast brown Gothic building. Within, the corridors were long and echoing. The endless stairways resembled the approach to a state ballroom. Hans placed his feet on the marble steps as though walking on slippery ice. He tried not to brush against anything. How lovely the light was. He remembered the diffused light he had once seen in a post-card of Chartres Cathedral. He could still respond to the sun and to the clean breath of morning in his nostrils.

Sophie walked beside him. She moved like a little girl balancing a book on her head. The imprisonment and the interrogation had left their mark, but her vitality held. He took her hand, as much for support as to help her. She spoke to him in a low tone. "I wondered if I'd ever see you again."

"It was a question whether anyone would. You know, Sophie, I've been thinking of ways of escape. I've been thinking of pleading for my life, and it makes me ashamed."

"But you haven't done it, Hans."

"No, I haven't."

"And you won't."

"No," he replied without hesitation. "I won't now, but I've thought about it."

Christl walked between Hans and the lawyer. His face no longer was puffy from weariness. Instead, the skin was waxy and drawn tight across the bones. He looked dead already. Neither Hans nor Sophie spoke to him. They knew he would prefer it that way.

Their lawyer seemed to take great pleasure in showing them the route to the courtroom. There were many public and private chambers in the building, he explained; more than they could possibly imagine. He was obviously proud of his place in the massive machinery of Nazi justice. Perhaps he was a good lawyer, Hans thought, but if they tried to flee, he would shoot them down as mercilessly as the guards who walked behind.

The courtroom was already filling up when they arrived. It had the garish beauty of a colored illustration in a cheap Bible. The spectators all seemed to be Party officials, most of them uniformed in black. The judges wore blood-red robes. The only satisfaction Hans derived from the scene was his parents' absence from the courtroom.

Before the trial began, Sophie told their lawyer, "If my brother is condemned to death, I don't want a more lenient sentence."

"My dear girl, what a negative attitude. I'm here to defend both your lives, even if you aren't."

"Did you have your toy replaced?" Hans asked him.

The lawyer looked at him the way a dog will listen to unfamiliar sounds. "Oh, yes," he said, remembering. "Thank you. I did."

"And did he like it? Your son?"

"Very much."

"But you couldn't do anything about your feet, I suppose. Do your son's, I wonder . . ." Hans never finished the sentence, for he heard the clerk calling his name. Conversation died in the courtroom.

"Hans Scholl, you are called before us to answer the charge of high treason."

Judge Dr. Roland Freisler presided. He was affectionately called "our Vishinsky" by the Führer, for his emulation of the Moscow trials of the thirties. He had the face of a vulture: all beak, with deeply-socketed, chaotic eyes. With conscientious venom he read the indictment.

"Hans Scholl of Munich, born in Ingersheim, September 22, 1918. Sophie Magdalena Scholl of Munich, born in Forchendberg, May 9, 1921. Christoph Hermann Probst from Aldrans near Innsbruck, born in Marnau, November 6, 1919. You stand before us for reason of traitorous behavior, giving aid and comfort to the enemy, preparing for high treason, and undermining the morale of the armed forces."

As Freisler went on to elaborate the charge, Hans caught only occasional phrases. Some of the more elaborate tirades were evidently designed to lash the defendents into a display of weakness. Hans found himself smiling involuntarily, a reaction not of enjoyment but of realization. He was seeing his first and final monster, the grotesque caricature of what he had all along stealed himself to fight. "You won't break down," he told himself. "You won't give them tears." They would enjoy tears. Show them honor. Show them a stony heart.

". . . the National Socialist regime has made it possible for Hans Scholl to enjoy eight semesters of medical studies, and this is his gratitude . . ."

Hans smiled. He was a defeatist, without a soldier's loyalty or honor. Still he smiled. Freisler's voice rose in pitch and fury like the warning hiss of a boiler that finds no adequate outlet. The other judges Hans never saw as individuals, although the lawyer had pointed them out to him: SS Group Leaders Stier and Bung, SA Group Leader Koeglmaier—those who would try him. They were like strangers on a streetcar staring at him in the dull hope of finding something amusing in his behavior.

"I will address the following to you, Hans Scholl," said the judge, "as I understand you were the prime

221

instigator of this conspiracy. Do you deny composing, printing, and distributing six leaflets to the German public, the contents of which incite to treason?"

Hans's attorney shrugged. How could it be denied? But Hans would not be still. "I deny any treason toward the German people." His voice was clear in the listening silence.

"You admit being responsible for the leaflets."

"I admit that."

"Then, Scholl, let the leaflets speak for themselves. Here, from White Rose leaflet number one, I read: 'Is it not true to say that every honest German is ashamed of his government today?' Not much there, surely! An opinion; ungracious, inaccurate, but nothing more. But then it goes on to mention passive resistance. What is this passive resistance? It sounds innocuous, but what of this, Herr Scholl? 'Obstruct the further functioning of this godless war machine before it is too late.' More ominous, wouldn't you agree? And here, in leaflet number two: 'Join us, then, by a last mighty effort. This system can be shaken off. An end with terror is better than terror without end.' What is that but reason? Of course the word used is 'system.' Vague, I suppose. Let us look further, to the next leaflet: 'How can I fight most effectively against our present government? The answer is by passive resistance.' Passive resistance again. But how passive is it to advocate sabotage in armament works and factories, sabotage in all branches of science? You wrote that, Scholl, and you cannot deny it."

He could not deny it. He had met Professor Huber by that time; Huber, who looked as if he belonged in the SS, but whose mind envisioned a future republic for Germany. Huber had become their oracle, without as yet suspecting a conspiracy. "There isn't any use cluttering our leaflets up with his philosophical visions. It's now that matters," Alex had said, and Hans had agreed in the beginning. The war effort must be hindered in every possible way. "What would you suggest?" Alex had commented. "Cutting buttons off the trousers of the SS when they're not looking? Kicking over milk bottles?" What was meant as a joke was painfully close to reality for activists without firearms or explosives; yet they had to try.

"You smile, Scholl," said the judge, with a peasant's heavy-handed taste of irony. "Good. So do I. Yes, leaflet four is quite amusing. It compares Hitler's mouth to the reeking portal of hell. Such imagery! Do you take drugs, Scholl? I think you must have been under their influence when you wrote that." It was Sophie's leaflet. The words were poetic, fanciful, but Hans had let it stand for her sake, and for an unknown audience they might not have touched before. "Let us pass over this rhetoric," continued the judge, "and examine the last two leaflets together. This statement to a nation at war, fighting for its life . . . tell me this isn't treason. 'A new war of liberation has begun. The flower of the nation are fighting on our side. Tear off the cloak of indifference that you have laid around your hearts. Decide before it is too late.' And this: 'There is only one watchword for us, war against the Party.' Let me ask you again, Scholl. Is this not treason of the basest sort?"

"We condemned only the Party, never the people," Hans told him.

"The Party! Only the Party. Your Führer is the Party.

Have you never heard that, Scholl? And he is the people, and the people are Germany. One flesh. Sit down, Scholl. You have condemned yourself. Sit down in your shame. If I did not despise your kind so thoroughly, I would pity you in your delusions. Sit down."

Sophie scorned to oppose Freisler's savage browbeating. She admitted everything, adding, "You know as well as I do the war is lost. Are you too frightened to admit it?" With his hands braced on the bench before him, Freisler leaned toward her. Irises of transparent blue crystal seemed to throw sparks as they caught the light. Sophie turned to the courtroom. "You agree with what we have said and written, but you are too cowardly to admit it." With her own tongue she demanded execution. As her words seemed to carry away the last chance of clemency, Hans loved her. He would remember that he loved her as he lay there, shoulders and arms tied, and the blade poised above his neck.

Christl alone offered a defense. "I'm only a family man," he said. "I'm not a political person. Even now my poor wife is terribly ill with childbed fever. I've been half mad with worry. Please, can't you see I never intended that writing should be published? Please, can't you see?" He could say no more, and it was left to their attorney to characterize him as temporarily insane and irresponsible; deranged to the point where he might be dealt with as a mental problem unfit to walk the streets, but surely not as a calculating traitor against the state.

Judge Freisler listened with evident interest, even with sympathy. Several times he leaned toward SA Group Leader Koeglmaier, and his lips convulsed in a wide rictus,

224

an imitation of laughter, but when he finally addressed himself to the accused, his words were full of contempt. "Let me ask you, Probst. Are you a man?" His voice cracked to the four corners of the room. "You stand there with your head hanging and keep silent. Very well, I will answer for you. You are not! You and your kind sabotage the victories of our Fatherland and then you ask for pity. Have we pity to waste on you while real men are dying on the battlefields without complaint? Without your privilege of studying medicine at the government's expense? Without the luxury of a wife or children to worry about?" The judge's voice had grown shrill as a girl's. "I answer, No! No, for all loyal citizens! We have no pity. What are you really, Probst? Look up at me! How can men sympathize with vermin? Sane or insane, you are vermin, and dangerous. You carry plague, and poison the public morale. Vermin must be exterminated! Sit down, Probst. No further proof of your guilt is needed here."

As Christl shuffled to his seat like a blind man, Hans could not bear to look at him, for it was through his own bungling that Christl was here. Hans's gaze shifted into the courtroom, and he noticed them for the first time. They had not been there when Christl had taken the stand, but at some time during Freisler's attack his parents had been given gallery seats. Hans could not clearly make out their features, but what he could not see he imagined. His father seemed barely able to contain his anger as he gripped the arms of his chair. His mother was twisting her handkerchief into a sweaty rope. Her face had shrunk since he had seen her last, and her hair seemed to have thinned away from her shiny forehead. He wanted to shout "Be kind to her!"—not because she was their mother, but because she looked so forlorn. For a moment his dreamlike insulation was stripped away. "Skin a cat!" her old bedtime refrain, came back to him; but it was his own skin now, not a boy's play-dirtied clothing, and the pain of it brought hot tears to his eyes. He would not give way. He set his features and tried to face his judges with scorn.

At the conclusion of the evidence, the defendants were allowed a final statement for their own defense. Sophie remained silent. Christl, looking ravaged and tormented, stood once more before Freisler. "I ask for clemency," he said. "Not for myself, but for my wife and children." And Hans, who had spoken no word in his own behalf, tried to defend his friend. "Christl Probst is innocent of any conspiracy. We alone, my sister and I are guilty." Finally their attorney offered Hans's and Christl's war records as mitigation.

The accused remained standing, but their lawyer sat down. There was an uneasy shifting of chairs, a pause like from an audience waiting for the orchestra to strike up. Following a very summary nodding of heads among the judges, Freisler began, "The accused have distributed leaflets, undeniably encouraging sabotage of the war effort and the downfall of the National Socialist way of life. Said defendants have encouraged defeatism, insulted the Führer, and thereby have given aid and comfort to the enemy. Against this overwhelming evidence they have offered one unsupported plea of temporary insanity, and war records no better than those of millions of German boys who are fighting gallantly and without complaint. Therefore, it is the unanimous judgment of this tribunal

226

that the defendants be sentenced to death. They have forever forfeited their honor and rights of citizenship."

The condemned stood like statues in pale marble. Despite the cold of his body, Hans felt a new repose, a relaxation of the will. It was over, and he had not betrayed himself.

Only details remained: their removal to Stadelheim Prison, from there to the place of execution within said prison, where their heads should be struck from their bodies. Finally, the cost of the proceedings were levied against them. With that, the trial was concluded.

The judges' chairs were already scraping back when Hans addressed one last sentence to them before they withdrew.

"Soon you will stand where I stand today."

His voice was not loud, but it was clear and steady, and reached every attentive ear. In the gallery, his father rose to his feet, square and big-boned, his deep-set eyes fierce and fearless. He bore his pride like a banner in defeat. But his voice, when it came, was not the hesitant cry of a beaten man. "There is another justice!" he shouted. The vibrant outburst had the authority of a bugle call.

Judge Freisler turned sharply toward the sound. His face was unevenly stained with color, as if cut by a lash. His mouth opened and closed. He made no reply, but rose and left the courtroom.

Herr Scholl might have shouted something more, had not his wife suddenly burst into tears and buried her face in his neck. She clung to him like a child, her whole body shaking, and they disappeared in the crowd.

Only Franz broke through to the defendants. "You're

227

raving mad, Hans," he said quite solemnly, and just as solemnly he took the other's hand and shook it slowly. Like victors they stood there. "At Stadelheim, Hans. Don't give up hope." There was time for no more, though no one hurried them. Among the guards there was a respectful silence. Finally one of the wardens asked Hans if there was anything he wanted to say to anyone. "No," Hans answered, and the policeman led them, very gently, away.

CHAPTER FIFTEEN

● They were driven directly to Stadelheim Prison, a route that traversed half the city. There were no road blocks to intercept them, no rioting students to overturn the car. They went unnoticed; deliberately so. The people on the streets were afraid of official cars. The jail itself was not a fearful place; it was even cheery, as prisons go, with direct access to the street and to nearby Perlacher Forest Cemetery, where several thousand anti-Nazis lay in a common grave. Once inside, the guards led them in darkness down long, gray-painted corridors lighted only here and there be small red bulbs, then up a stone staircase and down another corridor. Every few feet there was a cell door. Some stood open. Most were closed. Hans was left alone in a cell that glistened from a recent hosing. It had a table, a chair, and writing paper. From outside the guard switched on a single electric light. Then he closed the door, and spoke softly to the other guard. Their voices grew louder as their steps diminished.

Hans sat down on the chair. He would have stretched out on a bed if there had been one, but there was only the damp floor. Apparently he would not occupy the cell overnight. The paper and pen must then be meant to contain his last reflections on earth. There were people who deserved a letter, none of whom he dared write. Hans had always enjoyed writing letters.

Particularly in Russia, the moments when he had time to communicate with home had been important to him. Then he would try to carve out pictures of the space and wind and emptiness in that strange land.

The best days had been in early autumn, when the wind blew constantly, checked only by the small patches of woodland. Then horseback riding had provided a liberation he had not known since. The animal, too, had seemed to sense the turning of the year. It tossed its head as a heavy ripple of life moved ceaselessly through its reaching frame. How good it had been, alone with a horse again, and he had written of these happy times to Sophie.

Dearest Sister,

I will tell you the best thing I do here. When we have mended all the poor Humpty-Dumptys, I ride off like one of the king's horsemen. Yes, I have access to a horse. At first I had what passed for a steed; now only a nice old plug. I don't know whether he has a name, but I call him Napoleon, and we fare forth together before dawn whenever we can. I never knew the sun could rise in so many ways until I came here. It turns the sky pink, red, green, gray, blue. You would love to paint it. Hills appear slowly in the distance, row after row. The third range is usually green and distinct. A faint blue veil half conceals the fourth, and it all looks like a painting set up in cardboard on the edge of the world. Not far off there is a town with onion towers. I am watched by lemmings with jet-black eyes. They don't seem in a hurry; they just sit. Peasants pass. One must stay clear of them, for many, I'm told, are guerrillas in disguise. Except for a dead tank here and there with all its intestines spilled out, there is scarcely a sign of war. Well, I might go on and on without ever doing justice to the place. Perhaps one day, if there is ever peace, you and I, and maybe Alex, too, will come back as tourists. How odd that I should love it so. Most of my comrades despise Russia. I wonder. Is that because they feel like conquerors?

Writing might help to steady him now, but Hans had scarcely picked up the pen when he heard footsteps coming, marching fast down the corridor of stone and steel. His hands became tremulous and he expected the ink to spill from the pen, but the procession passed along the gallery. The jingling of keys reminded him oddly of sleigh bells, and he remembered how as children they used to go down through Kochertal for the caroling.

If he wrote no one else, he should send a final apology to his parents, but it was hard to write with handcuffs. Both hands had to move as one, clasping the pen as though it were a chisel, and the sheet of yellow paper a marble tombstone.

He had scarcely begun when they came for him at four in the afternoon. Hans stiffened, but it was not his life they wanted. It was something almost as hard. His parents were in the visiting room. Already he had hurt them irreparably, and things would have been easier said on paper. Now he must release them gently.

His father stood behind the barrier, scowling as though he would dissolve iron and stone with the power of his will. His mother had exhausted all emotion. She seemed to have mounted suffering and despair like a ladder into some higher calm. Her hand sought his across the barrier. She offered him sweets, but his stomach refused. "Come now, Mother. You don't want to spoil my appetite for dinner."

"We've appealed for clemency," she told him. "Hitler may commute the sentence."

"I'm resigned, Mother. It's all behind me, truly." He squeezed her hand. He had passed far beyond the point of outrage. Suffering, even the capacity for further insult, was in abeyance. He contemplated with curiosity the limit to which his anesthetized nerves could endure.

His father embraced him. "You will be part of history," he said.

"I don't believe history will be much concerned." In any case, that didn't matter. "I was writing you a letter . . . an explanation." He leaned across the barrier. Damn his eyes. They were wet. Hans kept his face down because of the tears. Wiping them away, he contrived a final smile. The warder was calling him.

"There's another justice," his father repeated.

His mother clung to him with her eyes and made the sign of the cross. In the deeper twilight of the corridor beyond, he put his hand against the wall to steady himself.

It was then that Sophie passed into the glare of the visitor's room. From the shadows Hans watched her. She wore her own clothes, for they had never been issued prison garb. Her face was alight with the passions of life and the proximity of death. She and Hans had tried to take complete responsibility, she told her parents. This had not helped Christl, but she had volunteered information to exonerate another friend. Confidently she predicted there would be no more victims. Wordlessly, her mother once again offered sweets, and Sophie accepted them. She had not had lunch. She was hungry. When the wardress called her away, she said, "What difference do a few years make, Mother?"

"There is Jesus, Sophie." Her mother's voice was barely audible.

She left them, smiling, her mouth full of candy.

Before Hans could call out to her, his guards prodded him along.

Hans expected no more visitors except the prison chaplain. When the door was unlocked, he was totally unprepared for the appearance of Franz. His white face looked unwell, and lopsided with an attempt at good cheer. It made Hans think of a snowman that had started to melt.

"Hans, I have only a few moments. If you repent now of your opinions, it may not be too late. There is just a chance of getting a reprieve direct from the Führer. Write, Hans, for God's sake!" He offered pen and paper, but Hans did not take them. He had been brought to Stadelheim to suffer death, and he was ready. "For the love of heaven, Hans! I'm risking my life!"

"I know you are, Franz. You're a good friend."

"Am I simply to call the guard, then?"

For a time they sat silently, facing one another. Hans only wanted to get on with the inevitable, as one who has

**233**

had a bad day looks forward to sleep. Franz stood up and sat down again. His mouth worked. "Hans," he said. "Hans, did you know this is a very special cell? Ernst Roehm died here. That's true. Look there, and there. You can see the bullet scars on the wall. Roehm was an important man, you know. He was the head of the SA. They gave him a pistol with one bullet, but he wouldn't kill himself, so they cut him to pieces, right here." Franz leaned forward and tore something from inside his shirt. It was a pistol. He shoved it into Hans's hand.

"Am I to kill myself?" asked Hans. "No, thank you."

"No, you're to escape."

"That's impossible! I'd be shot down in the corridor."

"There's a difference. You have eight bullets in there."

"Then in the corridor below."

"Please, Hans. Hear me out," said Franz. "I have a weapon as well." He patted the black holster at his side. "Part way I'll march you in front of me, as if you were under guard."

"Franz, have you lost your mind? We'll die in the streets, with dogs barking over us. Why are you doing this?"

"My friend, I don't know. I really don't know. I suppose I've listened to you talk too much. Oh, God, Hans! Come on! I have a car hidden. We'll make it. It'll be like old times. You remember, Hans. Switzerland, safety! We almost made it once before."

Hans had already envisioned himself escaping from Stadelheim and the implacable machinery of Nazi justice. With the flickering haste of an old Chaplin film, he had watched himself run down the corridor, down the stairs, out the door and over the wall as goggle-eyed, leadfooted

234

Keystone guards wrenched at pistols that were glued in their holsters. He was bound for the ends of the earth. A hedge-row blocked his way. He plunged through it, alighting on a brown lawn where white moths fluttered in a swarm of powdery wings. They swooped to escape, batting against his face. With pin-wheeling legs and flailing arms, he bolted through a ditch full of sluggish water, then rushed down a lane to a bridle path among trees. There was a sharp pain in his side. The ground had begun to rise, and he stopped for breath, seeing the mysterious hills before him. As he jogged on again, a forest rose up on all sides, and there was total silence: no shouts, no barking dogs. Then lights came on inside his head and walls stood all around him. He had a shivering fit, and held his arms tight across his body before the film could begin a second run.

"What about the others?" he asked. "Franz, what about my sister? And Christl?"

"I can do nothing for them. Sophie has no fear of the SS. They send her to God. At this very moment, Christl is being baptized. They are both of them before the gates of paradise, Hans. They will never know you aren't with them."

"But I'll know."

"If you had their faith, Hans, I could understand."

"Do you remember when you warned me about the Gestapo? That was only last week, Franz. I went to the cathedral then."

After Franz had left him, Hans had stood for a time in the rain. He had been near the apartment, but he couldn't face Sophie just then. Walking brought him to a square where windows had been boarded up because bombs had fallen there. On the far side, the church had loomed out of the mist like a great brooding hen with wings spread wide. Hans crossed the square and entered. No masses were being said. There was no reason why anyone should visit it at such a time. He walked down one of the side aisles and saw an old woman muffled in a shawl who knelt before the statue of an unknown saint.

The cathedral had been dark, the dull daylight scarcely illuminating the supporting columns or the three-paneled mural of Christ crucified, Christ buried, Christ risen. Hans felt a sudden pity for the tormented figure, as though it were some friend he had known long ago. Why was he alone? Where were the thieves? And where was Barabbas? Surely he should be there at the lower corner, making his way to another town.

Hans had studied the first picture only. It made him feel uneasy, like an unknown guest at a party who has been introduced to no one. Then he selected a pew and knelt down. He tried to think about God, but God slipped off into the shadows. His hands opened and shut. He tried to pray. "Oh, God, please help me. Convince me that what I'm doing is worthwhile. And if I have led the others into error, please, God, protect them." Daylight had vanished from the stained glass at the tall windows, but at the far end of the cathedral a large bank of candles flickered on the high altar. "God who is lost in the darkness, where we all are lost." He wanted a miracle, however minor. Not an Old Testament spectacle, but some small sign, here in the concrete, living world. But God had remained where he had always been for Hans, in the remote imaginings of childhood; a dusty God who could not help him now.

"What am I doing here?" he said aloud. "I've got to get out of this place. We've got to make plans." It was so dark he couldn't find the door. He tried following the wall and ended up in a side chapel, where he bumped into a tomb.

He might have stumbled about indefinitely had not a flashlight bobbed toward him. It was held by a large priest whose cassock flapped and billowed before him like the skirt of a medieval charger.

"Are you all right, my son?"

Hans nodded. "The light is very poor, Father. I don't know the way to the door."

"Did you come here to confess, my son?"

"I wouldn't know what to confess, Father."

"Surely everyone has something on his conscience."

He had been too weary to face a new venture that night. "I am not a Catholic, Father."

"Have you ever thought of becoming one?" The very fact that you are here . . ."

"One day, when there is time, perhaps."

"Yes. When there is time . . ."

The priest showed him the way to the central aisle. Go straight back, You can't miss it." He held up his light as a guide. Hans felt forlorn as he advanced, a solitary soul between the empty pews, with each ringing footstep taking him away from hope. There had been no hope there, not even in the dead figure of Christ upon the cross, nor in the grim stations depicting events that had happened long ago. He felt the priest's eyes following him. The vast darkness of the cathedral seemed the outer limit of what a human being could endure.

Outside, it had been raining hard. He had put up his collar and stepped into the street.

"There was no answer there, Franz. But I do have

one weapon left. The willingness to die. A few will understand."

"No one will know. You will have no grave."

"Franz, I am living a little already. I will stay alive; don't you see?"

"No, I don't. I see you dead, dead and buried in an unmarked grave before the sun rises again."

"But I am living, just a little, in you. I've gotten under your skin, Franz."

A look of despair had come into Franz's face. He would not take back the gun that Hans held out to him. Hans concealed it inside his own shirt. Franz's hands went to his collar, as though it were choking him. He tried to tear away the insignia, but they wouldn't come off. Then he knelt beside the chair where Hans sat, and crossed himself. "Please, Hans, pray with me."

"For my soul or yours?"

"For the love of God, Hans! A man can't go to his death alone. Pray with me now."

"Get up, Franz."

"Hans, please," he implored. "Holy Mary, Mother of God, pray for us sinners now and at the hour of our death . . ." He tried to pull Hans down beside him. Failing this, he began the Lord's Prayer.

"Franz, stand up. I have no need for daily bread. I would have to ask for much more than that, and I can't. If you must pray, pray for yourself."

The prayer had dissolved into incoherent sounds. "Get up, old friend. You're not going to die today." Hans pulled the trembling man to his feet as gently as possible, but Franz would not look him in the face. "It's all right, Franz. You've been my friend. No one could have done more." Quickly Franz recovered, drawing himself up inside his

238

uniform, straightening his collar. Whether he resented him for rejecting his offer or for observing his weakness Hans did not know, but it was obvious the interview was over. His leave-taking was short and formal.

"I take it, then, I can do nothing for you?"

"You might arrange a last meeting for the three of us, if you would."

"That's absolutely against prison rules, Hans. I'm sorry." He took Hans hand and shook it, but he did not again look into his eyes. Then he called the guard.

Hans assumed that was the end of it. But it wasn't quite, for within a few moments Franz produced a last demonstration of affection. An interview was arranged between Hans, Sophie, and Christl. Under guard, they met in the prison courtyard.

Sophie looked remarkably ethereal. To Hans she suggested the image of a medieval saint, animated, and the old love stirred in him. "Hans!" Her eyes shone, her whole face sparkled. But Christl's eyes were glazed and vacant. His face was pale as the death that faced him.

Together they smoked a last cigarette. Above them, framed by the prison walls, the sky was like the iris of an enormous eye. It stared impersonally at them. "It's been a beautiful, sunny day," said Sophie. "Like spring."

"It will be a beautiful day tomorrow," said Hans.

They talked like people who had met casually on the other side of the grave. Christl, already absolved, had been baptized by Father Speer, the prison chaplain. He had written his mother, and seemed resigned. His one regret was his family. "Poor Herta . . . the children." She had been too sick from the birth of their third child to be told of his arrest.

Sophie, too, had tried to arrange baptism into the

Catholic faith. Religious in spirit but never in practice, she had not learned those articles of faith prerequisite to baptism, and execution could not be postponed.

Hans held up his glowing cigarette. It was bright now under a sky from which the color was swiftly draining. It would burn a while and then go out, its life measuring his own.

Sophie related a dream she had had the night before. In the dream she had carried a baby in christening robes toward a cliffside chapel. Before she arrived, a crevasse had opened beneath her feet and she had barely managed to lay the child safely on the far side when she plummeted into the abyss. As she interpreted it, the child was freedom, and others would carry it to safety.

It could as easily represent her own cheated motherhood, thought Hans, but he did not say so. She already had one foot in heaven. He would not hurt her.

One of the guards called to them. "It's almost time."

"May we pray?" Sophie asked.

"Two minutes," was the reply.

With her head bowed and her face wearing an expression of calm remoteness, Sophie said the Lord's Prayer, then the Act of Contrition, and finally, "Hail Mary, full of grace, the Lord is with thee . . ." Hans tried to say it with her, but he was more aware of his burned-down cigarette and the elemental rhythm of his heart. The beat was that of a clock wound for fifty years more. "I am sorry, and I beg pardon," he murmured, not to God in contrition for his sins, but to Sophie and Christl.

Two minutes were spent. The guards edged closer, embarrassed to intervene, but under orders.

"We shall meet again, soon," said Christl. For him,

240

death was no longer a closed door, but one that opened upon the bosom of God.

By now the sky had lost all color. It was the hour when fathers return home from factories and play for a moment with their children, the hour when young girls find the first star to wish upon. There was a taste of spring in the air, but to Hans it did not matter. He understood now the apathy that precedes death and makes it tolerable.

He threw down his cigarette and ground it out.

They walked back between the guards.

"I'm not afraid," Sophie said, "but I just hate it. I hate it!" He took her hand. There was ice on the courtyard steps, and he did not want her to fall. Her fingers seemed icy, too. Their coldness chilled him. "Harder," she said. "Squeeze harder. I can't feel my body."

Once more they were returned to their separate cells. Hans's cell was dark. The light bulb had burned itself out, and the young moon printed the shadows of the bars on the wall. He went to the window to look at the moon and to see if the mountains were visible. They were not, but the wind had stopped blowing and the air was so sweet he could taste it. Below, evening sounds were creeping up from the other floors of the prison. There must be a kitchen not far away, and his stomach gurgled because it was empty.

He would have stood by the window tasting the night until they came for him, but the chaplain was admitted and he had things to say. Hans tried to explain that he simply wanted to be left alone. "Surely not, my son. In these trying moments, you must be afraid." Of course; he admitted that. "Then God can help you. All men turn to God in their hour of travail."

241

"Father, I'm sorry. I've been through this so many times. You can't help me."

If he must die, he wanted to do it in his own way. For what he had done, he wanted to share neither blame nor credit. In the process of complete divestment that the last days had forced upon him, he had reached the final indivisible element: I am. That was all, and when it was gone, there was nothing. He was reconciled.

The chaplain dropped his eyes and sat down. They remained together in silence until the chaplain rose. "I am truly sorry," he said. "I must visit the others."

"Father," Hans asked, "would you do one thing?" The priest waited. "Dispose of this." He handed over the pistol and the priest took it, searching Hans's shadowed face for a clue. Then he left without a word.

Presently, with a ringing of keys, an SS detail marched down the gallery past his door to another cell. Hans heard the command to halt, the sharp, clean report of a bolt being drawn. He was at his own door now, looking through its small window. The marchers were returning more slowly, and Sophie was with them. The chaplain was beside her, and there was a Bible under her arm marked at the page where she had stopped reading.

"Good night, Sophie," he called to her.

"No, Hans," she called back. "Good morning."

"Silence!" ordered a guard.

"As they reached the door at the end of the gallery, she called again. "God bless you, Hans."

The door clanged shut and the sounds resolved themselves into silence. Hans returned to the window and pressed his face against the bars. He gazed at the glimmer and haze of the moonlit night. Beyond the prison roofs he

242

could see the tallest pines of the Perlacher Forest. The other way lay the city. He could imagine the river there, his beloved Isar with its green-brown banks and the swamp mist rising in swirls.

He listened against his will for the sound of metal striking flesh and bone. Supper was being served to the prisoners, and perhaps he had missed it amid the clatter of tin trays. The time had surely passed. Sophie would be with the river now.

Then he heard the footsteps tramping up the corridor again. The guards and the chaplain marched by quickly. They called Christl from his cell, and returned very slowly. The chaplain supported Christl by the elbow as he shoved one foot after the other, like bags of sand. *"Indulgentiam, absolutionem, et remissionem peccatorem vestorum tribuat vobis omnipotens et misericors Dominus . . ."* The chaplain's recitation carried down the gallery like echoes from the back of a church.

Hans waited for the last time with the sensation that he was no longer in his cell, or rather, that his cell was no longer composed of solid substance. He existed apart in endless empty corridors of air, and his mind was so fixed upon this perception that he did not hear the footsteps in the corridor. The door opened and the light poured in. "Sophie," he said, but it was only the light that dazzled him. The guards walked on either side. They did not touch him. His feet were steady enough and did not lag, but when he came to the first flight of metal stairs, he lowered himself slowly the right foot always going first, like a child's. His hand sought the rail. Bulbs recessed at regular intervals illuminated the whitewashed walls. A blue line at shoulder height went the length of the vaulted passage.

They came to a door at the end of the corridor. Before it was opened, the chaplain took hold of his wrist.

"Please, don't touch me," Hans said.

They entered. A black hose lay uncoiled on the floor. There were puddles of water, and in the center of the room stood the squat black engine with its long neck. It was smaller than he had imagined from pictures he had seen of the French Revolution. He closed his eyes. They were tying him down, and he held himself rigid so that it might end without his ever uttering the great cry that was tearing him apart. Then he was flat down. He heard the sound of rollers, and at the last there burst from his throat a cry, uttered in a great voice, a voice that combined anger, reproof, and an overwhelming conviction for which he was willing to die.

"Long live freedom!"

Then the greased blade fell. His teeth met through his tongue, and it was over.

● Their cells were empty; they had left nothing behind. They were buried that night in Perlacher Cemetery. The Scholl family was present, and the prison chaplain told them, "Greater love hath no man than this, that he lay down his life for his friends. We are in darkness now, but the sun will rise again."

The following day the newspapers briefly mentioned the execution of three deluded eccentrics, and a rumor went around that Hitler had sent his personal pardon—too late. Other members of the family were imprisoned under the Nazi law of *Sippenhaft*, which punished people for the crimes of their relatives.

Throughout the University the news spread. "Yesterday the Scholls were executed for treason." One had known all along Hans was in for trouble. He had lived too long with a single dream. But Sophie . . . "So quiet and pretty." "She never said much outside class." "They say she was the most defiant of all." "What could have set her to break her

245

body so young?" "Last week she sat in that seat right there . . . no wonder she was so strange. She must have thought of herself as Joan of Arc." "Well, I hope they don't give you ideas. Keep your head down and your mouth shut; that's my advice."

There was no revolt, though the Gauleiter was hooted at by students, and on the walls of many Munich houses the inscription appeared, "Scholl lives! You can kill the body, but never the spirit." "Germany's Enemy Number One" was scrawled below Hitler's picture in the University assembly hall. The unrest was sufficient to result in a committee of students and professors loyal to the Party that checked up on the others and sent those of questionable patriotism into war work or to the front. Still, the story lived. British leaflets, dropped from planes, spread it all over Germany almost as Sophie had imagined.

They had tried to take all the blame and punishment upon themselves and had died hoping that they had been successful at least in this. But within the next few days, Professor Huber was taken into custody. Alexander Schmorell, who could not endure the lonely mountain life, returned, and in a Munich bomb shelter he, too, was identified and taken. They were tried in April. Professor Huber, conducting his own defense, quoted from Johann Gottlieb Fichte:

> And thus you are to act
> As though the destiny of German life
> Hung solely from your deeds, and you,
> And you alone were accountable.

On the twenty-first day of April, 1943, Professor Huber

246

and Alex were condemned to die. Willi Graf, another student who had spread leaflets in the Munich area, was found equally guilty. Eugen Grimminger, who had given money to the cause, was sentenced to ten years in prison. Students who had distributed Hans's leaflets in other cities received less severe penalties: Heinrich Bollinger and Helmut Bauer, seven years; Hans Hirzel and Franz Müller, five years; Heinrich Guter, nineteen months; Gisela Schertling, Katherina Schuddekof, and Traute Lofrenze, one year.

In July, Kurt Huber and Alex Schmorell were executed. In October, Willi Graf followed them. It was said that all died with Christian resignation.*

Other trials were held in secret. A number of SS personnel at Stadelheim Prison were put to death for reasons undisclosed. It had been suggested that they had been influenced by the Scholls.

One way or another, the principals were punished. In February of 1945, a bomb carried away a Berlin courthouse where Judge Freisler was presiding over the treason trial of Fabian von Schlabrendorff, who had placed a bomb, unfortunately defective, in Hitler's private airplane. The courtroom and the trial papers were destroyed, and Judge Freisler, hiding in a shelter beneath the courthouse, was killed by a falling beam. Only the defendent survived the war.

Bombs destroyed the Wittelsbacher Palace in Munich, where Hans and Sophie were interrogated. Later the de-Nazification trials sentenced Jakob Schmid, who had arrested Hans and Sophie, to five years of hard labor. It

---

* The characters presented here, with few exceptions were real. Among the principals only Franz Bittner is fictional.

fined Albert Scheithammer, the Secretary who had turned them over to the Gestapo, two thousand marks and set him free.

Hitler died in his Berlin bunker, but before he held the pistol to his head, he recorded in his last will and testament: "I die with a joyful heart in my knowledge of the immeasurable deeds and achievements of our peasants and workers, and of a contribution unique in history of our youth that bears my name." He would be remembered, but with no monuments other than the crude parking lots fashioned from bomb craters, the concentration camps restored in cement, and the graves.

The square before the University of Munich was renamed Scholl Platz. Today one may see the likenesses of Hans and Sophie carved in stone inside the University's great front hall. And it is not solely in stone that they are remembered. Rival student groups have fought for the right to bear their name. In Ulm, their elder sister, Inge Scholl, has founded a flourishing school, dedicated to the principles for which Hans and Sophie died.

They are remembered. But in terms of their objective, the overthrow of Nazi tyranny, they did not shorten Hitler's dictatorship by one day. Were their lives wasted then? They seemed doomed from the start, and they accepted that doom and rushed toward it as though it could not wait. Did their narrow choice between impossible victory and death explain their fervor and serenity? There was something childlike about them, and this trait only made them more lovable. They were too solemn in their grandiose pretensions, and perhaps a bit naïve. Those who struggle to save their moral identities from the fire always are. But if their lives were squandered, there was perfection in their dying. They took nothing away with them except the unmarketable consciousness of having done what they ought to do in spite of pain and fear; that which sentimental people might degrade by calling it glory, but which is glory all the same.

Very little remains of Perlacher Forest. Munich has grown enormously since the war. But Stadelheim Prison has survived, as has the nearby cemetery. The custodian of Perlacher has few visitors, but he knows the Scholls, row and number, by heart, and will mark them on a cemetery map. Then you may wander through the silent shade past forgotten names and nameless markers until two iron crosses stand before you, joined by a single arm. The names are in marble there, Hans and Sophie Scholl, *Geschwister Scholl*. No longer separate, but an entity and an ideal.